JOHN MCGRATH
RESPONSE

CW01501280

PROLO

It had been a steep learning curve for ~~~~~~,

understand how hard being a police officer was they might have a
different view of them. The training was mentally tough with so much
to remember, especially the law and how to apply it in practice. Then,
once the classroom phase had finished it was another steep learning
curve putting into practice what you had learnt. Ten weeks with a tutor
to put into practice what you had learnt in the classroom before going
'independent' and dealing with crimes on your own.

You never stopped learning and every situation you dealt with was
different. The public's view of the police from all the various TV
shows was probably nonstop action, flying around in a police car at
100mph.

The actuality is far different from that; there was the mountain of
paperwork for each arrest, the equation of 4 hours of paperwork for
every 10 minutes of action was not far from the truth. The various
forms that needed to be completed to build a case up ready to submit
to the CPS. The number of forms could amount to up to maybe 11
different forms, some several pages long. These included an overview
of the offence, evidence, witness lists, disclosure and if the suspect
needed to be put on remand - a flash word for being kept in prison
whilst awaiting trial. Someone being punched three times in the face
could take an entire hour shift, to get a witness statement, gather
CCTV, create a crime report, interview the suspect, and any other
statements required.

The most important form is the MG11 witness statement, which could be several pages long and often handwritten. The average statement taking one and a half to two hours to write. Then, on the reverse side, you could spend nearly all of a nine hour shift patrolling the area with no jobs coming in – although that is getting more and more of a rarity.

Whilst statistically most crime is undertaken by teenage white males, it is still assumed the criminal fraternity was made up solely of the types found on the 'Trisha' or 'Jeremy Kyle' television shows. Whilst true to a point, James had arrested an Earl for theft, a large company director for ABH, a war veteran for child pornography, and a middle class housewife for attempted murder, to name a few.

It could be dangerous at times; James had yet to be assaulted, but many of his colleagues had suffered a thick lip or bloody nose. Thankfully, no one had been killed in James's force for quite a few years. The number of firearms offences committed each week had gone up from 'just a handful' 30 years ago to more than 230 and still rising. James had been told gangs were using Kalashnikov rifles and machine pistols able to fire 40 or 50 bullets in rapid succession.

In 2005, PC Sharon Beshenivsky was shot during a robbery at a travel agent in Bradford, West Yorkshire. Then, in 2012 PC Ian Dibell was shot and killed off-duty whilst trying to protect the public. In September 2012, two female police officers, PC Fiona Bone and PC Nicola Hughes, were shot dead by Dale Cregan, who not only shot dead the two officers but also threw a hand grenade during the incident. He later drove to a local police station and handed himself in

for the double murder. In October 2015 PC Dave Phillips was run over and killed by a vehicle trying to evade capture.

As a police officer, James's life was never his own, being under scrutiny 24 hours a day. This even involved the monitoring of his and other cop's Facebook and Twitter accounts to ensure they did not bring the service into disrepute. Then out on the streets in uniform, Joe Public loved cops when they were moving on a group of rowdy teenagers in their hoodies - then loathed them when a cop arrested them for drink driving. When giving Joe Public a ticket for speeding, cops are quite often asked why they are not catching, "real criminals" like rapists and murderers. This interesting love-hate relationship is something James has never been able to fully understand. There were always those people that hated the police for no apparent reason. Indeed, even a light hearted conversation for a polite request ending up becoming more of a heated conversation. James was never sure to blame the media or the government or both for the image of cops, similar to that of a dodgy car salesman.

At the police station, cops were monitored frequently, with every keystroke they made on a computer being logged. Sadly, as James had seen during his service, it was at times needed, with a handful of corrupt cops selling intelligence and supporting criminal gangs in return for money or drugs.

James had been in the job several years and in that time seen it all. From the cop who was afraid to get involved in any form of altercation and would hang back going to a fight or any violence, to the criminal mastermind who robbed his local convenience store, wearing a pair of boxer shorts over his head. The disguise was so poor that the shop owner was easily able to recognise the criminal mastermind.

Violent incidents were always interesting simply due to the unpredictability of them. James could go to a call of youths fighting and find no one, and then on another occasion be called to a disturbance at a local charity shop and end up in a fight. Domestics were probably the worst for unpredictability, as they could start quite calm before getting more and more heated. Often the police would be in the middle of an argument and were often used by one partner trying to one up on the other. One elderly man who was known for being nice and kind, one day snapped in an argument and threatened his wife with a knife.

Neighbour disputes were another interesting aspect. Neighbours often believed the police would be able to sort it out or again be able to use the police to get one up on the other neighbour. Once, James got called to a dispute, where, on his arrival everyone had calmed down and they had all wanted to make a complaint about each other's foul language. The moment James pulled up, the first neighbour moved so quickly his pants must have been on fire, wanting to be the first to make an allegation. It wasn't before long that the next person in the queue stepped forward and made their allegation, and so on. Indeed, almost immediately the first male started shouting, "I want him fucking arrested for being a twat." James did his best to explain that was not an arrestable offence, to which James received, "You're fucking shit, and the police are fucking shit." After a section five public order warning or swearing, he calmed down. James, then spent two hours doing all the paperwork, talking to everyone and being a mediator. It worked well for about a week - before the same neighbour called out the police for exactly the same reason James had been called out.

The squalor that some people would live in had taken James back initially; where the street outside was cleaner than the carpet inside the house. The state some people would let themselves get in was simply unbelievable, even in custody when they would wet or crap themselves. One prisoner had a crap, then proceeded to wipe it across the walls of his cell.

James had been called to a road traffic collision where a car had driven into the side of another parked car. On arrival the male driving the car that had crashed jumped out his car and admitted to drink driving, followed by:

"Officer, can we get this done quickly, I need to get myself sorted. When I crashed, I shat myself and have a giant log in my pants that is fucking uncomfortable."

The drink driver was very compliant and came quietly. The difficult person was the owner of the parked car who was understandably annoyed. He decided it was the fault of the police and was both arrogant and unpleasant to James's colleagues, even though they were just trying to help. That was the nature of police work, with more often than not nothing being as it seemed.

Cops, themselves could do the silliest of things too, like the story of when a probationary officer was searching for a suspect, after a burglary. The camera operator radioed to the officer that he had seen someone acting suspiciously in the area.

However, he failed to realise that it was actually the plain-clothed officer, he was watching on the screen. The operator directed the officer, who was on foot patrol, as he followed the 'suspect' on camera telling his colleague on the ground that he was "hot on his heels."

The officer spent around 20 minutes, giving chase before a sergeant came into the CCTV control room, recognised the 'suspect' and laughed hysterically at the mistake as he realised it was one of his officers.

Then there were the horrific accidents you often got called to, in particular road traffic accidents, which could be akin to being in a war zone with limbs that had been severed or large quantities of blood on the road or inside a vehicle. You could go to a severe-looking crash and the car looked totalled and everyone was fine, or what looked like a relatively minor crash and you were dealing with a fatality. The smell of death was something that you never forgot, especially a body that had been left decomposing for a few days or weeks. Over 21,000 elderly people die at home alone each year, often not found for days, weeks or even months.

The worst smell James had ever smelt was that of burning flesh from a fatal car fire. A woman in her twenties had left the road and ended up in a ditch. The car had caught fire and there was nothing anyone could do to save her or get her out. The real tragedy was that when the fire brigade inspected the remains inside the car they noticed some small bones. It was later confirmed she was twenty weeks pregnant and her baby had died in the accident as well.

James had seen the government cuts bite and the force sent into dismay following the Windsor report; good cops made to retire under the A19 rule only to be replaced two years later with some rookie cops. Then budgets cut with the loss of 17,000 police officers and a further

17,000 police staff. Quite a few cops had retired on ill health grounds or simply resigned as morale hit rock bottom..

Being a cop was sometimes the best and the worst job in the world, but one thing it was never short of was variety. Being part of a close-knit team and the banter was what got you through a bad day. The camaraderie was very similar to when James had been in the Army, and was one element he enjoyed in both.

During his years of service, James had been spat at, punched, kicked and had several people throw up on him. Only once did he have the pleasure of being covered in human excrement, but more about that later...

PART ONE - FIRST DAY BLUES, 2010

After 18 weeks of training, that had been quite mind blowing in places, learning everything from suspect interviews, self-defence training to using the various computer systems and mobile data devices. James pulled up to the main entrance to the police station with a slight squeal from his car's front brakes. He swiped his brand new warrant card at least five times before the main gate decided to open. The gate opened slowly with a loud creaking noise as James began his first day on the front line. The police station was quite a new square shaped, brick building, with three floors that replaced the previous old police station made up of three houses joined together, which had stood for over forty years.

James could remember cycling passed the old police station as a young teenager on his way to the shops. Watching the police officers come and go, some running out to their panda cars, some just strolling out on foot patrol. At that time, he never dreamt that one day he would actually be a response cop himself. He had watched cops in their Ford Escorts race to emergencies with the single blue light flashing and the distinctive Ne Na, Ne Na sound that has now fallen into history. His only previous encounter with the police had been aged 16 when he got into a fight. It was the night before a GCSE exam and one of his mates was being picked on. James had decided to wade in to help his mate and ended up in a full-on fistfight, his reward being a black eye. The police decided to take no further action as the other lad involved who had started the ruckus had actually come off worse, with a bloody nose and two black eyes.

James was now in his early twenties; he was quite tall with floppy brown hair and green eyes. He had been to university to study a degree in civil engineering. Unable to find work after graduating, he had sold cars amongst other jobs before applying to join the police service. Selling cars was more of an occupation than a career. Getting free fuel and regular new cars to drive was a real benefit of the job though. James had become addicted to that new car aroma. However, this had to be offset by the hours of boredom during the week with very few customers, then the long hours and six-day week he had to endure.

He had never been a high achiever and had just plodded through school and scraped through his A Levels. The only reason he ended up going to university was that his mum, exasperated with James having no plans for the future, got in contact with the local university and got him a place through clearing. He had just managed to srape a 2:1, although he nearly failed his first year due to poor attendance and not really putting enough effort in.

James parked his rather tired and battered 2002 Ford Fiesta complete with scuffed alloys and a large dent in the driver's door. His car was one of the first things to be replaced as and when he had some spare cash. However, having just bought a brand new flat not too far from the police station, money was a little tight. The sales woman had been very good at selling the flat, maybe too good, making it all sound so cheap and simple. It did not work out quite so cheap with a ten per cent deposit, legal fees and then a loan from his parents for the shortfall. Then finally, James needed to furnish his new flat. He was in debt before he even started paying for the flat. At least he had his own place and no more arguments with his younger sister over the bathroom.

The weight of all his brand-new kit, weighed James down. James wondered how he would be able get in and out of a police car, let alone run. His basic kit consisted of a stab vest, utility belt with its extendable baton or ASP, handcuffs, high visibility jacket, waterproofs, gloves and even a small first aid pack. The final piece of kit was the distinctive police helmet, otherwise known as the custodian or "tit," although this only had to be worn when out on foot patrol. James dragged the kit from the boot of his car with a hefty tug. He then managed to shut the faulty car boot with a hard slam. Before he made his way to the changing rooms.

James's heart started to race a little as first day nerves started to take over. Once he found the locker room, he found a locker with a key in it and a Post-it note on the front saying "James Sowman." The tall grey locker only had just enough space to fit all his spare kit and kit bag. It took two attempts to get the rather stiff lock to lock properly so he could take his key out. Swearing at the lock must have told it who the boss was. He slipped on his police shirt before putting on his utility belt and sliding his ASP into the holder on his belt. Finally, he put on his stab vest.

The stab vest had to be the correct size for each officer and consisted of two main, Kevlar inserts and two smaller ones on the shoulder. These would need to be replaced every five years to ensure they still offered full protection. Initially there were quite bulky to wear as well as quite warm. James had tried it on at home a couple of times and found it a bit uncomfortable, although it did have useful pockets for putting in his pocket notebook, tickets, pens and some latex gloves. James also found that the nifty LED torch he had just brought fitted perfectly into one of the loops used to clip other equipment on.

Once ready James made his way to the parade room; it seemed to have taken forever to get changed, fiddling about with his new epaulettes that had already been wrong. They had been made with 3468 J Snowman instead of 3468 J Sowman sewn on them. People were forever assuming his surname was Snowman, not Sowman.

In the parade room, James gingerly clipped his shiny new radio onto his brand new stab vest trying not to hit the orange emergency button on the top which was all too easy to do; a reassuring click meant it was held securely. Then finally, he shook his CS spray and popped it into the holder on his belt. Everyone used to call it 'Gas' until it was challenged in court as a defence and the offender got off. Since then everyone has been told to call it a spray or better still incapacitant spray. In reality the actual CS element is just a crystal, which in the CS canister is suspended in what is basically an industrial paint stripper and propelled out by nitrogen gas. The paint stripper was to ensure that when it was sprayed into the eyes the paint stripper removed all oil from the skin, so the CS crystals could get into the pores around the eyes and cause the desired irritation. The one issues with CS is that it is highly flammable and even a spark from a taser can cause it the CS to burst into flames on the individual being restrained.

Finally, he managed to clip his radio on even though his hands were shaking with nerves (which only made this simple task harder). James's Sepura radio was more like a mobile phone than a radio, using a system called Airwave. The Airwave network is a mobile communications network dedicated for the use of the emergency services in the UK. Designed to be both secure and resilient it allows multiple agencies integrated communications through a nationwide network. It is a secure digital, encrypted network and can be used for voice and data transmission. The radio had GPS, text messaging, the ability to type in another officer's collar number like a telephone number and talk to them direct. They were not without their issues, though, with poor atmospheric conditions lead to a weak signal, and to the operator they sound like you were talking inside a biscuit tin. On the whole though they worked well and were a good bit of kit.

James had heard stories of student offices not clipping on radios or other equipment and on the first run after an offender suffering an "equipment burst" with radio and other kit flying off in one direction and baton in another. James sat down and waited for the start of the 7am briefing, which was nothing like the American parades as depicted in the 80's TV show 'Hill Street Blues' with twenty cops and the immortal words 'be careful out there' said at the end. James's shift was now four people, including James and a sergeant. It could drop to three or two if someone was off on holiday and another pulled off for an operation or football match.

James heard a voice behind him "Hello James."

It was the voice of his tutor, Constable Lauren Reilly. James recognised the voice instantly as he had only spoken to her on the phone last week. He had been quite surprised by her soft and calm tone on the phone; she was not how he had expected a police officer to sound. James's perception was that a police officer is all tough, gruff and very assertive. This quite softly spoken and pretty lady was not what he had in his mind a police officer would look and sound like.

Lauren was quite tall and thin, but had a lovely reassuring smile that would melt a million hearts, and teeth almost so white you could see your reflection in them. Her long blonde hair was tied up in a bun and her blue eyes twinkled

"Are you ok mate? Once we have done briefing we will sit down and have a chat before going out on patrol," said Lauren.

James nodded and gave a shy smile as he slumped down like a defeated boxer.

The briefing room was the size of a small living room with a single table and chairs around it. There was a projector and screen on the wall. On the walls were various pictures of local criminals; some young, some old. It was a veritable rogue's gallery with details of the offences they had been charged with. The offences ranged from shoplifting to burglary to serious assault. These were the criminals to watch out for, then either arrest or gather intelligence on.

Then James noticed out of the corner of his eye, the bizarre sight of a worn car tyre that looked like it had suffered a blowout or something, as there was a big hole with bits of wire poking out. Underneath a note read, "This is why you should check your tires regularly - good job nobody was injured." Inspector Moon had signed the note. It was a tyre off one of the police cars, which had suffered a blowout during a chase due to excessive wear.

In the briefing room was Chris, who was in his early thirties with wavy dark brown hair and a slight tan. He was making various slurping noises as he tucked into a bowl of cornflakes and milk, just before briefing.

In walked Sergeant Bloor, quite a stocky bloke with hair just starting to go grey, and it was cut short on the back and sides. He walked in and said, "Morning" in a gruff tone. His chiselled looks were unable to raise the faintest hint of a smile. People had told James about Sergeant Bloor and that he could be rather standoffish, but looked after his section well. He was known to be a good skipper and had the most amazing knowledge of the law.

Just a minute after, the Sergeant walked in, followed by Ian looking out of breath - as if he had just run a marathon. Ian was very tall at 6" 4', with shortly cropped ginger hair. His police t-shirt was hanging out and his trousers looked as though they had never seen an iron.

Sergeant Bloor barked, "I see you are late as usual PC Collins, and looking at your uniform you have yet to get it washed from your last set of shifts!"

"Sorry skipper" Ian replied in quite a dull tone almost as if he was expecting it.

Sergeant Bloor, then said, "Seeing as you're late you can go and do us all a brew." Ian did not reply, he just got up and shuffled his way out of the briefing room to make drinks for everyone.

"Right, let us get on with the briefing," barked Sergeant Bloor.

"Firstly, I need to introduce you to James Sowman, who is joining the shift and being tutored by Lauren Reilly."

Ian sparked up from outside "Snowman? That's a funny name."

"Shut up Collins, get them brews in here" retorted Sergeant Bloor.

Ian then shouted "Snowy do you want tea or coffee?" James replied, "It is Sowman, and tea please" in a slightly frustrated tone. "Milk and sugar?" Ian said, "Just milk" James replied.

Sergeant Bloor said, "Let us introduce you to the rest of the shift, James. "This is Chris Theakston" who had by now finished slurping the remaining milk out of the bowl of cornflakes. "Lauren you know, and the shift joker Ian Collins is outside making a brew. I will have a chat with you later, but for now just get settled in and go out with Lauren."

Ian strolled in with four cups of tea, plonking them down on the desk, hard enough for some of the tea to splash out onto the briefing table.

The big screen on the wall burst into life. The screen was filled with an intelligence program which showed all the local intelligence, including photographs of people wanted or to keep an eye out for. One woman, a prolific shoplifter and drug addict, looked twenty years older than her age suggested. She looked all haggard and wrinkled like a prune from the effects of years of drug abuse.

Sergeant Bloor, then scrolled through a series of pictures and information until he stopped. "Here is a new one. Steve Turnbull has been released from Shardlow prison, used to be a prolific burglar round here and on B division. Keep an eye out as he is still local to the area."

"Ok, we do have a handover from the night shift, Chris that can be your call?" You could tell by the look on Chris's face he was not happy. James knew what a handover was as it was covered in one of the many lessons at training school. James remembered it was when someone had been arrested for a job that the previous shift had not been able to complete and required further investigation. The handover had all the paperwork completed so far and a note on what still needed doing.

"What are the plans for the rest of you, Ian?"

Ian replied, "I have an IP to visit and a bail back at 2pm." James again had to think IP, bail back. Like any job the Police is full of acronyms. James again remembered that IP meant Injured Party - the person who had been the victim - and bail back was when someone was coming back to answer the result of a charge after they had been arrested. Then all the investigation into the crime had been completed. A decision was then made if there was enough evidence to charge the person with an offence.

"What about you Lauren?" Sergeant Bloor asked. Lauren replied, "Well, I have some paperwork to finish off so I can go through that with James before going out on patrol." Lauren smiled at James in a knowing manner. James thought, "Is there something I should know?"

With briefing over everyone seemed to leave and find the nearest computer. James sat a little bemused for a few seconds and then decided to do the same, wondering what exciting emails he would find in his inbox this time.

The biggest surprise for James was that just three cops would cover a 100 square mile area with a population of about 70 thousand. How could so few cops cover such a wide area?

Just as James finally managed to open his email after what seemed like hours for the computer to whirr into life and load everything up his radio broke into life. "DC to Alpha Romeo 377" there was a short pause and Lauren said, "Alpha Romeo 377" to which control replied "I have an immediate come in on the A27 near Campbell, serious RTC, three cars involved and injuries reported. Ambulance and Fire are travelling." Lauren replied, "Show us travelling." At that point, James thought he had better get ready to go to his first job and a serious road traffic collision as well. "Come on James" Lauren shouted across the parade room.

Lauren and James made their way to the police car which was a fairly new Ford Focus estate and already with some minor battle scars.

"Chuck your stuff in the back James and let's get going."

Within minutes they were making their way towards the A27 near Campbell, blue lights flashing and travelling quite fast. Cars moved out the way, although others required a blast of the siren to move. Lauren shouted at the car in front, "Get out of the way" as if the car in front would reply. The blue lights bounced off shop windows, making James feel he was travelling in a mobile discothèque.

James's heart was in his mouth on a couple of occasions as Lauren overtook cars on the wrong side of the road. The cars coming in the other direction just kept coming with no sign of them actually slowing down, even with blue lights flashing and the siren wailing away.

They finally made it to the A27, and traffic was already building up when over the radio came "DC to Alpha Romeo 377'" Lauren replied "Alpha Romeo 377" We have an update that it is a serious RTC and potential fatality, can you start running a log please."

James thought, "My first job and my first shift and I go to a fatal RTC." His mind raced, wondering what he would see and what he would do. They had covered RTC's at training school, however, not what to do with a fatality. How would he react? What would he do?

In the distance, James could see three cars, with one facing towards them, but he could not work out what make or model it was even though he was a bit of a car geek. As he got closer, the severity of the accident became apparent. There was a sea of blue flashing lights twinkling in the dawn sunlight. He could see two of the cars were almost totally wrecked, and the front end of one had been destroyed.

What was left of one front wheel had been pushed back to the driver's door. There was glass, water and oil all over the road. One looked like an old Vauxhall Astra and the other a Saab 93. The third car, a Ford Kuga 4x4, looked fine with no damage to it. A scene of total chaos seemed to be in front of him with people rushing around and others sitting down talking in small groups.

The ambulance service was already on scene; busy assessing the casualties. One casualty was laying in the road, "where had they come from?" thought James. Lauren stopped the police car and placed it across the road with lights flashing. She pressed the run lock button and removed the keys, so the engine would keep running to power the blue lights without fear of someone stealing the car. James sat motionless, not quite sure what to do. It was a scene of carnage with possible fatalities. He remembered the visit to the morgue during training when he went light-headed and nearly fainted. Thankfully he managed to grab onto a workbench, avoiding any embarrassment.

Lauren shouted "Come on James, we need to get stuck in" using a stern tone. James got out the car and the flashing blue lights of the police car almost blinded him. He walked slowly towards the two wrecked cars, still unsure of what to do or say. The two occupants were out of the Saab, and in the Astra, sat motionless, a female face stared out.

Lauren went to the paramedic and asked what the casualties were like. He pointed to the car with the motionless female in and said, "She is a goner, nothing we can do. This one on the floor, she is barely with us after being thrown through the car windscreen. I have requested the air ambulance and we need fire to free the dead female. Two more are walking, and just sitting over there with a member of the public whilst another ambulance arrives."

She got straight onto the radio to control "Alpha Romeo 377, we have got one fatality, another possible and another two injured, going to need the Tango Papa's and the road closing" Tango Papa's was the radio term for the Traffic Police. They would always undertake the investigation of a serious or fatal accident, which involved either death or life changing injuries. With serious and fatal injuries, the accident site was now a crime scene and a cordon needed to be put in place to prevent any potential evidence being lost.

Just as Lauren had finished, another fire engine followed by an ambulance pulled up and came to a stop. The fire fighters leapt out and went to assess the scene followed by another two paramedics. James was still stood motionless, trying to take the horrific scene in. He needed someone to tell him what he should be doing. He felt sick and overwhelmed to the point that he was frozen to the spot.

"JAMES" shouted Lauren "GET OVER HERE!" This prompted James into action; he still felt sick as he made his way over to Lauren.

"James, I know this is a bit of a shock, but can you go over to those two sitting by the side of the road to try and find out what happened?"

Meanwhile, the fire brigade began unloading all of their equipment, whilst talking amongst themselves about the best way to get the casualty out of the car. James had got to the casualties sitting at the side of the road with a member of the public comforting them. James said, "Hello, err, sorry to disturb you, err, just need to find out what happened and, err, take some details."

James felt nervous and could not remember any of his training at this point. It was as if his brain had been emptied of anything useful.

The first casualty was a man in his 60s, who looked fine at first apart from a slight cut to his head. He had a very pale complexion with sunken eyes and was shaking like a leaf.

He spoke softly with a slight croak "I was just driving along at around 60mph when a car just seemed to appear in front of us like it had pulled straight out in front of us. There was nothing I could do… It was all so sudden, and we hit the car head on."

James noticed that across the road was a petrol station. He wondered how on earth they could have pulled out the wrong way.

"OK" James replied, "Can I take your name and address?" The man replied "Jack Sanderson, 45 Main Street North Allenton" "Err… Ok, thanks, we may need to speak to you again." James felt pleased he had actually done something and made his way back over to Lauren who was now speaking to the fire brigade

By now the traffic police had arrived along with Chris from the shift to help with scene preservation and closing the road off. Control had been onto the council to get the road closed between the island half a mile down the road, and a main junction that a diversion could be put in place. The rush hour had already started, and traffic was building up.

The road would be closed for hours, maybe even most of the day, whilst investigators studied the scene and took photos. The highway agency would need to put a diversion in place.

James waited for Lauren to finish before saying, "I have got the driver's details."

"Was he ok on the breathalyser'?"

James replied, "Err, I did not ask"

"Ok, I will go and do that, seems that the Astra pulled out of the garage the wrong way and headed down the dual carriageway the wrong way. That person on the floor went straight through the windscreen, obviously not wearing a seat belt. As they had been thrown out they had crushed the driver, killing them instantly."

James said nothing as he tried to take it all in. He couldn't help thinking that only she had worn a seatbelt, then maybe she could have walked away and maybe the driver would have survived.

A whirring sound could be heard overhead as the air ambulance arrived. By now, the road had been closed off in both directions so the helicopter could land easily. Paramedics were still working on what looked like a bundle of clothes. The bundle was actually the other female from the Astra who had been thrown through the windscreen at 60mph. The impact of hitting the windscreen at speed and the impact with the road had seemingly squashed her. She was in a very bad way indeed.

As soon as the helicopter landed, the doctor and paramedic rushed over to assess the casualty. They asked if James could help get her into the helicopter. James hesitated again, unsure of what he would see and did not want to faint in front of all these other emergency services, never mind his own shift.

James took a deep breath and wandered over to the casualty where he could see drips, lines, and an awful lot of blood, to the point that it was hard to make out the face. However, James could see blood stained brown curls coming out of what James thought was her head.

The doctor shouted, "Are you ready to move?"

The doctor looked in his forties, but it was hard to tell with his white helicopter helmet on. Everyone confirmed that they were. James was at the feet as they made the short distance to the helicopter where the casualty was placed into the back. With the casualty on board, the helicopter was off and within a few seconds had disappeared out of sight on its way to the Kings Royal Hospital. The noise of the helicopter left a deathly silence, apart from some light chatter from the various emergency service personnel.

Lauren was with the casualties from the Saab and managed to get a breath sample out of the driver, Jack Sanderson, on the back of the Ambulance. The breath test was negative, confirming alcohol was not a contributing factor to the accident. It seemed they were just in the wrong place at the wrong time. Thank goodness the road was not that busy; a half-hour later and there could have been an even bigger pile up.

Jack explained the other car had come out of nowhere and hit them head-on, and he was doing around 50mph at the time. The force of the impact had caused his car to almost jump backward and ended up at 45 degree angle to the road. The Astra had not taken the impact quite so well and thrown a female passenger out of the window and onto the

24

road. This had caused severe head trauma as well as a whole host of internal injuries as she hit the tarmac at high speed. The driver of the car who had been killed, other than a few minor cuts looked relatively unscathed.

Jack Sanderson and his wife Silvia were taken to hospital for a check-up and treatment for shock. Things could have been a lot worse for them and the car had done a good job of absorbing the impact, even if it did now look in a very sad state. The fire brigade had cut the roof off the Astra so they could remove the body of the dead female inside.

Lauren asked James, "Can you do a PNC check on both cars?" PNC was short for Police National Computer, the first thing James had remembered. James went to the back of both of the crashed cars and got the registration numbers. PNC holds details of anyone that has ever been arrested and then taken into police custody. The vehicle element hold all the details of UK registered vehicles and any foreign vehicles that are of interest. A recent addition is in insurance details. You can also check UK driver licences on PNC as well.

James hesitated and rehearsed what he was going to say before he clicked onto his radio and said. "Alpha Romeo 377, err, can I have, err, a vehicle check at this, err, accident, I mean RTC."

Control replied, "Alpha Romeo 377 pass your details." James then looked down into his notebook and read out,

"The first is Delta Uniform 56 Sugar Hotel Oscar." James realised then Sugar should really be Sierra. He had learned the phonetic alphabet perfectly, but the nerves of using the radio had got the better of him.

Control came back "The first is a Saab 93 in black registered to a Jack Sanderson Main Street North Allenton and there is insurance to view, pass the second." James replied "Romeo 476 Golf Tango Victor." Control replied, "That comes back as a Vauxhall Astra registered to a Michelle Watkins 45 Broomfield Avenue Birmingham showing MOT expired and no insurance.

It was then, that it all dawned on James that the dead woman in the car was real. He walked back to Lauren and said "I have done the checks, the driver of the Astra is a Michelle Watkins - she lived in Birmingham."

Lauren replied, "Have you checked her for ID then?" James replied, "No."

"Go over to the ambulance over there, where Michelle has just been placed into and see if there is any ID on her. Also, check to see if there is a handbag or any ID in the car."

James really did not want to go and ruffle through a dead woman's pocket, so he went and checked the wrecked car first.

In the passenger foot well, there was indeed a brown handbag, quite a trendy one James thought, and similar to an expensive handbag his handbag-obsessed ex-girlfriend had brought. Inside James found a purse, and among various credit cards and discount cards was a driver license, but to James's surprise was green with a big red L in the corner, meaning it was a provisional and not a full license. The name on the card was a Michelle Watkins and this really brought home how real this all was.

Michelle had not only killed herself, but also seriously injured another from a lack of experience and pulling onto a dual carriageway the wrong way, even though there was a barrier in the centre and the petrol station could be accessed from one way only. Now James felt angry at the lack of thought Michelle had shown to others. Her car still needed to be checked by a police vehicle inspector to see if the mechanical state of the car was a contributory factor as well.

Back at the police station, a rather white-faced James sat down to collect his thoughts as the shock of what he had just dealt with began to hit home, when Chris came up and said,

"Don't worry mate, I have seen worse."

Chris then told James a story of a bike accident he had been sent to a few years ago. A member of the public had handed him a bike helmet that they had found lying in the road after the accident. When Chris turned the helmet over which felt slightly heavy for a motorbike helmet he found the head of the victim was still in it. The force of the impact of the motorbike crashing against the crash barrier at over 70 mph, had literally ripped the motorcyclist's head clean off. Chris was first on scene and had not initially seen that the body slumped over the crash barrier had been decapitated. The strange part was the complete lack of blood anywhere and that the motorcyclist had not suffered any other visible injuries.

James was not quite sure how this was meant to make him feel better, rather it just added further to his anguish and wonderment of he would cope next time. James still felt sick and that his stomach felt as if it had fallen to his knees.

CHAPTER TWO – THE SMELL OF DEATH

James was into his fourth week and third set of shifts, the two days of 7am until 4pm then a further two of 3am until midnight had not been too bad. However, the 10pm until 7am had been a bit of a shock to the system. Staying awake on the first night shift was the hardest, as his eyes seemed determined to close and stay closed. It took a great amount of effort just to keep them open. He felt fine until about 4am when a wave of tiredness washed over him. Then by 7am, he was too awake to go to sleep. Sometimes coming off a busy late shift at 1 or 2am he would find his mind racing and difficult to switch off.

James had been affected by the tragic car crash on his first shift four weeks ago. Sadly, both the mother and the daughter had died in the end. The daughter died on route to hospital of multiple injuries. They had left behind a grieving husband and father. James had felt sorry for the cops in Birmingham that had to go and break the bad news. It had hit him hard and had made him wonder if he was cut out for being a police officer.

Although, James was slowly finding his feet and confidence. He realised that being a police officer was not just about arresting people or flying around with blue lights on. You often took the role of a mediator or a social worker trying to resolve situations. The ability to be the voice of reason and placate a volatile situation was all part of the job. It was far easier to try to reason with someone than getting into a fight. Most people reacted well to just being polite and explaining everything, not getting agitated or frustrated with a situation and simply remaining calm.

Only last week he had spent three hours at a house trying to resolve a dispute between neighbours. Both neighbours had got on really well until three weeks ago. Dave Hadley had apparently ignored his Polish neighbour when she was out pushing her daughter in the buggy near home. It had been unintentional, but was the trigger for a much larger dispute.

Angelika had then ignored Dave on another occasion, and later when Dave came round complaining about damp coming through on his wall, she felt like he victimised her. All Dave had wanted to do was help them remove soil from behind the wall to fit a membrane to prevent damp seeping through his wall. He had even offered to do all the work himself and pay for materials.

Dave could be a bit sharp at times and no doubt, Angelika was a bit rude back and refused, saying it was her land he wanted to dig up and she did not want the plants destroyed. Angelika's husband Steve had seen Dave in the garden and had a heated conversation, and Dave had accused Steve of assaulting him. Angelika had accused Dave of making racist comments indirectly when she heard him say, "Foreigners should all go home." The problem had still not been resolved even though Lauren got the Neighbourhood Police Team involved, and they had tried to arrange mediation.

The problem actually got worse and two years later, James leaned that Angelika and Steve had decided to move, after Steve had suffered a breakdown and allowed his baby son to fall off his own knee without doing anything to stop him. The stress of the situation had caused him to begin to unravel and social services had become involved. Enough was enough and it was time to move, much to Dave's delight as he had won. Sadly, the next neighbour if he crossed him would probably suffer the same fate and pressure, as Steve and Angelika.

James had come in a little early before his shift started at 7am to get some paperwork finished, a statement from a drink driver whom they had pulled over on their last night shift. With it being a Monday morning, he had to endure the emails with the latest knee-jerk reaction from a senior rank. Often these contained ideas or directives, and whilst sometimes good, were also more often than not used to help career progression at the expense of frontline cop numbers being reduced to add numbers to an operation.

He had followed a van with Lauren, which seemed to be driving erratically down the road, and when they reached a suitable place they put the blue lights on to indicate to it to stop. The van pulled over and stopped before then reversing back slightly and just nudging the front bumper on the police car.

James went round to the driver's door to ask the driver to hop out and join him on the pavement.

His breath smelt heavily of alcohol, and as he got out of his van he stumbled and struggled to walk in a straight line, slipping on the muddy grass verge. He was in his 50's with round silver-framed glasses and curly grey hair, quite slim but about 6 feet tall.

James had to steady the male whilst Lauren went and got the breathalyser to test his breath. The reading came back at 52, so he was over the over the prescribed limit of 35 micrograms of alcohol per 100 ml of breath. The male seemed quite compliant until it came to the handcuffs. He was having none of it as James fumbled trying to get the quick cuffs on. Lauren had to come and help as the man swore and contested the need for handcuffs.

Handcuffing to the rear was a requirement for the safety of officers, after the tragic case of an army staff sergeant Steven Graham. Who killed a police officer when he pulled on the handbrake of a patrol car in which he was being carried to police cells. The police car was being driven by PC Joe Carroll at 70mph along the A69 near Hexham, Northumberland, and flipped over during the crash killing PC Carroll instantly. Steven Graham was heavily in drink and had been cuffed to the front.

It was James's first arrest and he had got a little bit nervous giving out the caution.

"You do not have to say anything, but err it may hurp your eer defence if you mention somthink later and"

James then started again.

"You do not have to say anything, but it may harm your defence when questioned later something you do not mention, anything you do say may be given as evidence."

He felt elated, but the man just stared blankly. It was his second time being caught in the past six years. He had driven less than half a mile from the pub in his works van to his home were James and Lauren had stopped him.

The man was placed in the car and as soon as James and Lauren drove off, he was swearing like a trooper. "You're a fucking cunt do you know that, I pay your fucking wages and all you can do is put these fucking handcuffs on, I will tell you now that when they come off I will kill you, you fucking little cunt." then almost at the click of a finger he started to cry. James made a note of everything he said in his pocket notebook as evidence if required. James had been quite shocked at how drunken people behave. They can go from happy to sad, then just as quickly become violent and abusive.

James had written an arrest statement on the night, but Lauren said it was not detailed enough so she had told him to re-write it.

"I am a Police Constable 3468 SOWMAN of Hampshire Police currently stationed at Otherton.

I was on duty in full uniform on 7th September 2010 at 23:30 with Police Constable 466 REILLY when we saw a white Van VRM KY57KWU being driven erratically and weaving along the road. We followed the car from Main Street to Fairburn Drive when we put on blue lights, and the van pulled to the side of the road.

On opening the door to the van, I could smell intoxicating liquor on a male who I now know to be Elliot NASH DOB 23/04/59. As NASH got out of the van, he stumbled and was unable to walk in a straight line. PC 466 REILLY breathalysed him and gave a reading of 52. I handcuffed NASH to the rear and CAUTIONED him for driving whilst unfit through drink or drugs.

NASH made no reply to caution, and we conveyed him to the custody suite where his behaviour continued to be abusive saying. "You're a fucking cunt do you know that, I pay your fucking wages and all you can do is put these fucking handcuffs on, I will tell you now that when they come off I will kill you, you fucking little cunt." By the time we got to custody, NASH became compliant. "

James hoped this new statement was now good enough. He had just finished the statement when Lauren came in, not yet in uniform, wearing a pair of tight-fitting jeans and a yellow top that really showed off, her recent holiday tan and blonde hair.

It was the first-time James had seen Lauren out of uniform.

"Hiya James" said Lauren,

"Hi, I have re-done that arrest statement could you have a look at it after briefing?" replied James.

"Yes, sure hope it is up to scratch, so I can sign it off in your PDP."

James had been given a big folder full of tick boxes that need to be ticked and initialled by his tutor, for his Professional Development Portfolio or PDP for short. The most important part of it was to be signed off as competent for a whole variety of tasks. From simple ones like using the radio and planning where to go on patrol to more complex tasks such as putting a file together for the CPS.

He had managed to get quite a few of the basic items signed off, but really his first week had been spent just soaking it all up and watching Lauren go about everything as if she had been doing it all her life. He had felt so overwhelmed at times with so much to do and remember. TV shows made being a Cop seem so simple but failed to show the mountain of paperwork and procedures you had to undertake. The ten minutes of action followed by four hours of paperwork.

James logged off the computer and went into briefing.

The Sergeant was already sitting down and Chris as always, had been eating, the giveaway was the food stuck to his chin. It seemed a bit too quiet in the briefing room today. The only conclusion James could come to was Ian not off work today. Ian was a nice bloke even if a bit silly at times. Other cops were not quite so keen and thought he was not very good at his job one saying, "Ian is just a security guard living the dream" which got quite a few laughs in the parade room. James had not really worked with Ian other than on a couple of jobs they had been to when he came as backup and seemed switched on.

Part of being a cop was putting up with the banter cops did like nothing more than to have a moan every now and again along with ribbing each other. Then the odd practical joke thrown in for good measure was a good way to let off steam with the more serious side of the job.

Briefing was the usual run-through of local hot spots and people to keep an eye out for. Lauren had brought some cakes in for everyone, so that kept the banter down to a minimum. It was hard to crack a joke with a mouth full of cake. James was still rather quiet and only spoke when asked a question. James did not want to sound stupid or silly in front of the rest of his shift.

After briefing, there was the usual scramble for your 'favourite computer' before the morning shift started to come back in off patrol. James sat next to Lauren, so she could check his statement and sign off some more elements in his PDP. James had to do everything twice to be deemed competent at it. So far, James had done quite well and managed to get pretty much all the basic stuff signed off. Lauren had been pleased with his progress so far and told both James and the skipper he would make a good cop.

The downside was it made him feel; under more pressure to do well and not make mistakes. James and Lauren spent a good hour doing paperwork with Lauren running through various forms with James.

The morning shift had come in and gone home after a bit of the usual banter mainly aimed at Ian Collins. Some cops from another shift had given him the nickname, "Calamity Collins" due to some mistakes he had made in the past.

The funniest being when he had tried to pursue a group of people suspected of dogging, he had then driven straight into a field and the police car had gone down a ditch. James did feet this was a bit unfair as Ian had been so helpful and very approachable. The nicer nickname was panda as once when he was out on foot patrol a few years back a group of drunken girls had come up and given him a big hug and said.

"You're just like a giant panda really sweet and cuddly."

From then on the name stuck.

Out on patrol not much seemed to be happening all, "QT" as it was called instead of the word "quiet" which was banned from said whilst on duty. The word "quiet" was considered tempting fate to mention it on duty, as it usually had the reverse effect once mentioned. James and Lauren visited the usual hot spots and pulled up on a layby on the A27 only a mile from the fatal crash they had attended only a couple of weeks ago. As soon as the car came to a standstill, the radio suddenly burst into life. "Alpha Romeo 377 can you make your way to 129 Stanton Avenue a neighbour has just phoned in to report they have not seen the old man who lives at 129 for over a week, and his household rubbish is causing a very bad smell."

Lauren pulled the car onto the A27 and made their way to the property. As they pulled up to 129 Stanton Avenue, it did look very quiet; curtains upstairs were closed with no lights on. Lauren walked up to the door and banged heavily on it. She asked James to go round the back and look through the windows to see if he could see anything.

Lauren banged hard on the front door and got no response, she then opened the letterbox and was just about to shout when this horrible smell of rotting garbage hit her, out of the corner of her eyes she could see some flies buzzing around. Lauren pretty much knew that she would be dealing with a sudden death. She shouted to James to come back round to the front, before she kicked the door open with such a force the lower pane of glass shattered.

Lauren knew, instantly, that the male of the house was probably dead due to the very pungent and sickening smell along with the flies she could see upstairs. James checked downstairs, and Lauren made her way upstairs. She simply followed the smell that got stronger and stronger as she got closer.

As she swung, the door open to the bedroom, Lauren could see a body lying in the bed, it had already started to decompose and there was a small amount brown liquid on the floor. The room was full of flies buzzing around - Lauren shouted for James to come up stairs, whilst she got on the radio to give an update. She would still need to get a doctor to certify death before the undertaker could come and take the body away.

As James walked upstairs, he felt his stomach churn again, just from Lauren's tone he could tell what she had found. The smell really did make him cough and feel sick, he was not looking forward to what he was about to see.

The smell was so bad, James and Lauren decided to go outside and get some fresh air whilst they awaited the doctor and undertaker. Who would take the body to the morgue for an autopsy. It looked as though the old man had died in his sleep, as there were no signs the house had been broken into. So seemed it was most likely not a suspicious death. Although scenes of crime would have to come out just to double check, so until then the house was a crime scene.

Thankfully, the doctor was there quite quickly. Lauren had asked James to go and have a chat with the neighbours to find out when they last saw him and if anything suspicious had happened. Everyone was both saddened and shocked by his death, as he was well liked and often stopped chatting to people. It made it even stranger as to the length of time his neighbours had allowed before becoming concerned.

Once the doctor had certified time of death scenes of crime began in the bedroom. Once scenes of crime had collected any evidence, then undertakers could move in. Lauren had made sure James only stood at the door and she had not ventured any further to ensure any valuable evidence was not disturbed. Once James had finished chatting with neighbours, he returned and stood outside in the late-afternoon sunshine, which was quite warm being late spring.

James and Lauren stood chatting away enjoying each other's company whilst scenes of crime did their bit taking photos and checking for clues. Next, it was the undertakers turn had the grim task of removing the remains. They were both more than happy to stand outside, whilst they got on with it. Lauren knew that a sudden death required a quite substantial coroner's report filling out along with a mountain of paperwork. However, it would be very good practice for James and at the same time was grateful to have James to help her.

By now, they had been at the property for nearly 3 hours, both of them were ready to go and get some tea as their stomachs made gurgling noises and pangs of hunger could be felt. Only last week, James had just sat down to eat his microwaved curry and an immediate came in asking them to go and deal with a road rage incident. James then came back to a cold tea that could not be reheated again, without most likely giving him an upset stomach.

When they could finally leave, Lauren asked, "What have you got for snap?"

James replied "Nothing"

Lauren then said, "I'm mad for some chips and a fishcake, local chippy ok?

James replied, "Yep, no problem usual policeman's tea then?" Lauren just laughed.

On the way to the chip shop, yet another call came in this time to a girl who had just smashed a shop window in Stanley village.

It was a slightly longer drive down a dark twisty road to get to Stanley. On arrival they both caught sight of a girl matching the description of the offender.

Lauren pulled into a car park, and James jumped out before the car had come fully to a stop. The girl spotted James and ran across the road, James managed to catch up with her, though. As he got close she just grabbed and hung onto a lamp post.

Lauren was soon with him and said.

"Hello Claire, not seen you in a while?"

Claire Hall was well known to the police, she was constantly in trouble for criminal damage, theft and ASB. She came from a broken home and was currently living with foster parents in Stanley. Many of the crimes she committed were purely for attention.

Claire was 15 and quite tall for her age; she had long curly brunette hair and green eyes that were wide open with excitement from being chased by the police.

Lauren arrested her and they took her into custody, when asked to empty her pockets, Claire simply took off her boots and trousers. Under her trousers, she had leggings and thick tights so must have had some common sense to keep warm on a cold day.

James got talking to her and said. "What do you want to do when you finish school? Any plan's college, sixth form?"

Claire replied, "I want to stab my hand and then have been shot by the time I am 16"

There was not much James could say to that, Claire was obviously a very troubled girl and James did feel sorry for her. Lauren got Claire booked into custody and would need a responsible adult to be interviewed. They also had the crime report to fill out, contact the shop owner and do a handover.

By the time, they had finished all the paperwork it was home time and the grey sky turned to a black sky with heavy rain. Although still late afternoon the journey home had been spent peering at slowly moving red lights from cars and a gentle patter of rain on the car roof. Now, as Lauren turned off the ignition and everything went dark. She stepped out into the wet evening air as she walked up to her front door. The path was thick with slippery leaves that had fallen from the tree in the front garden. The detached house was a welcoming sight.

Lauren rattled the key into the lock tilting it to the particular angle, which would allow it to catch. Lauren would be moving out soon and could not be bothered to get it fixed. She stepped inside her hand brushing the light switch as she closed the door behind her. The softly lit warmth of the interior walls was a welcome contrast to the dark slimy surfaces of the outside. The house was quiet and a stark contrast to the hustle and bustle of the police station.

Lauren lifted the carrier bag onto the worktop full of shopping, she had brought on her way home and she reached for the kettle. Standing in the centre of the room still in her anorak she listened to the sound of the water boil and just stood motionless. The house did feel empty and Lauren hated coming home to an empty house.

Steam began to rise to the ceiling, as the kettle came to the boil and Lauren got on with the task of adding milk and a tea bag to a mug. Through the window, she could see the outline of the narrow garden and the fuzzy grey shapes of a rusting climbing frame and overflowing wheelie bin.

Lauren reached up to the top cupboards for the tea bags. She took off her coat and laid it over the back of the oak kitchen chair before sitting down. She finally got round to taking her trusty Lowa boots off. Lauren then placed them onto the fitted bench across the other side of the table ready for a polish and a clean later. Above the bench were shelves supporting an array of holiday mugs picked up from various destinations, and a collection of family photographs.

Lauren unpacked the carrier bag, she put away the milk the orange and the biscuits. Then finally, she struggled to slide the two pizzas into an already crowded freezer spraying ice across the floor, as she tried to close the freezer draw. An overflowing collection of polythene bags scrunched inside other polythene bags at the bottom of a cupboard was her commitment to recycling. When the cupboard door was opened an avalanche of plastic bags slid towards her. She threw in the latest addition and quickly slammed the door shut.

With a cup of tea made, Lauren went into the living room, sat down on the sofa, curled up and put the TV on. There was nothing that she really wanted to watch, so decided to watch Downtown Abbey, which she had recorded three weeks ago and had not yet managed to get round to watching. Halfway through she felt her eyes getting heavy and fell asleep on the sofa.

CHAPTER THREE – THE CHASE

Whilst booking a prisoner in at the custody suite, a woman decided to strip off and run around naked. In order to protect the woman's modesty, Lauren pushed her into a cell with the aid of a detention officer. Friday and Saturday nights were always busy in custody, with many of the 'residents' being a bit worse for wear after taking various substances. Some would shout abuse, some would sing, and some would cry whilst they waited to be booked into custody.

James had still not managed to get his head around how different people could be after they had been drinking. They could go from normal, decent, friendly individuals, to the ones who were obnoxious and quite violent. They could be even more difficult to handle than a very stroppy teenager. They would often shout and scream, then lash out and become totally unreasonable. The slightest thing, even just asking them their name, could cause them to kick off. An intoxicated person was the one type of person James hated dealing with the most, and he was always happy to have a few extra cops on hand in case they kicked off.

The prisoner James was booking in, was an arrest that CID had asked the shift to affect for a robbery at a petrol station some weeks earlier. The main offender had been caught and charged. It was the getaway driver they had been sent to arrest. Once booked in, Lauren and James went back out on patrol to enjoy a "Friday night of fun!"

Out on patrol, they had the usual mixture of jobs, such as anti-social behaviour from teenagers, and a minor domestic caused by an argument that got a bit too heated.

"DC to Alpha Romeo 377."

Lauren replied, "Go ahead."

"I have a report of an immediate domestic at 27 Knightsbridge Close."

"Show us travelling."

The blue lights went on and Lauren and James made their way to the address. Due to previous incidents at the address, Chris had offered to back them up.

Lauren had explained domestics to James; she had said on many occasions, especially during domestic disturbances, people want the police officer to be the referee. They know they will step in if things get out of hand, so they use this as a chance to say or do things they would not normally say or do. All too often, this leads to an explosive situation. A cop is not always aware of what is going on until it is too late and ends up having to react quickly. Some basic points to consider are not putting the violent offender in a kitchen with knives to hand and ensuring both parties are in separate rooms, so you are able to talk calmly without interference to find out what has actually gone on.

On arrival, they found out this particular domestic dispute was between a husband and wife who had been separated for some time. This was not the first time the police had been called to the address. The couple had been having domestic troubles for years.

As Lauren got out of the car, she saw Chris coming down the street. She waited on him, as she knew the male could be a handful and could well need three cops to control him. The husband opened the front door and invited them in, being almost too polite. The door opened into a modern-looking living room. Straight ahead was a large flat screen television against the wall. The couple had three children, aged from about six years to a girl of fifteen. The children lived with their father at the address. The mother had decided to move out and was just visiting.

Once inside, the husband said he wanted his wife removed from the residence. Lauren asked him what was going on and he stated that he had custody of the children. His wife had come to pick them up for the weekend, and they had all gone out to dinner together. During dinner, they'd had a couple of drinks and one thing had led to another; by the time they got back to the house, they were arguing. He held out what he said was a harassment notice stating that, until their case got to court, neither of them was to bother the other. The paper in his hand was ripped into little pieces. He said his wife had ripped it up when he rang the police.

Lauren told him it did not matter whether the paper was ripped or not because she was not going to try to enforce it. Harassment orders could be tricky in the best of situations and, in this case, they had violated it. The husband had invited his wife round, thereby making it void by the invite because it had been consensual. Chris then told them both that a harassment order was made to keep people apart so trouble would not start. It could not be forgotten until trouble started, and then selectively enforced. Lauren told them that if the wife was going to take the children for the weekend, why not take them and arrange a neutral drop-off point? That could solve the problem. Lauren could tell they were both getting agitated so she split them up. Chris took the husband into the dining room and Lauren stayed with the wife in the living room.

Once the husband had left the room, the wife then informed Lauren that she could not leave because he had taken some leads off her car so it would not start. Lauren went and asked the husband about this, but he said it was not true and totally denied it.

When Lauren was back with the wife, she started out with the same old line about how they had not been able to make their marriage work, and it had progressed to the point where he had become a bum. "Totally useless and was not fit to take care of the children." She made out to be the wounded, hard-done-by wife; nothing was her fault and she was just trying to be a good mother. While she was talking, she was standing in front of the television facing Lauren.

Then whilst talking to Lauren, the woman said, "He's angry because he's afraid when we get to court I'll say something about him having sex with his own fifteen-year-old daughter!"

Lauren had her notebook in her hand, taking notes. Somehow, the husband had overheard the conversation and decided to push past Chris and race into the living room. He hit his former wife with a right hook to the jaw, which knocked her sideways onto the television, sending it crashing to the floor. Lauren dropped her notebook and pen as the husbanded jumped onto the wife and tried to grab her around the neck.

Chris was close behind. James, at that point, was out at the police car getting a domestic pack, and unaware of what was happening inside the house. Chris was not fast enough for Lauren; she threw the man out of the lounge door at Chris. They both landed in a heap on the hall floor, and Lauren dived on top of them. Chris had been caught off guard, but had reacted quickly and grabbed the man from behind. He wrapped

45

one arm over the man's shoulder and around his neck and then, with the other arm, he tried to grab hold of the man's right arm.

Chris tried to get both his arms so Lauren could handcuff him. Lauren heard Chris scream and looked up to see that the man had Chris' hand in his mouth and was biting it. Lauren slammed her fist into the side of his arm as hard as she could, right on a pressure point; this caused him to release his bite. During all this, the six-year old boy was running around swatting at Lauren and Chris, yelling for them to leave his Daddy alone. James had finally heard the commotion and come running back to try and help.

After several more minutes of struggling, Lauren, Chris and James got the man handcuffed and under control. The man was arrested for GBH, resisting arrest, and assaulting a police officer. James also located the missing ignition leads to the wife's car under the seat of the husband's car. James put them back on the wife's car for her and made sure she was not hurt. They then took the husband to the custody suite. He was still quite agitated in the car, making threats and trying to raise his arm up to James, who was sitting next to him. James pushed his arm back down and told him firmly to sit still. Lauren decided to use the blue lights to get to custody as quickly as possible and have a "welcoming party," which meant extra cops or custody staff helping get the man into custody.

It was just after 11pm when James and Lauren were finally able to head back to the station after having taken a statement from the wife, and they now needed to do their arrest statements for the husband. However, they had been diverted to a village for a report of anti-social behaviour, but when they got there could not see or hear anything and marked the job off as "no trace." As they were heading back to the nick, they saw Ian with an articulated lorry stopped on the right side of the road, going the same direction as them. Ian was standing at the cab looking up at the driver.

As they got closer, they could see Ian climb up on the step of the lorry cab. He then jumped down and ran to his police car. Lauren slowed down to about 30mph. As she passed them, she noticed that the lorry was slowly moving away from the curb.

At first, James and Lauren did not know what was going on; they thought Ian was just extra motivated, and could not wait to get back on patrol to write another ticket. Ian was quite fond of traffic type stuff and giving out tickets. Ian had not realised that James and Lauren were there and got on the radio.

"DC, this is Alpha Romeo 275. I am in pursuit of a lorry. He's running away from me!" Ian was out of breath from his run and excitement. "I am on the B56 heading towards East Waltham."

Lauren still did not really understand what had happened. "Maybe, somehow, the lorry driver did not realise Ian was not finished with him, and had started to pull away," she thought. Lauren slowed down in front of the truck and turned her blue lights on so the lorry driver would stop again. Lauren called into control and told them where she was and that she was assisting Ian.

Lauren then heard Ian again talking to control. He was getting more excited now, screaming into the radio, "DC, he's going to hit Alpha Romeo 377. Tell her to get out the way!"

Lauren was still slowing down, trying to get the lorry driver's attention. She looked into her rear-view mirror and realised she was the one Ian was yelling about.

Lauren took her foot off the brake and slammed it as hard and as far she could on the accelerator, pushing it to the floor. The police car started moving forward as she saw the front bumper of the lorry just inches from the rear of her car.

As Lauren pulled away from the lorry, she came to the A27. The truck turned left onto the A27 without slowing down. Ian, by now, was following. Lauren had to turn around and fall in behind Ian.

All the reports to control Lauren and Ian had done over their respective radios had led to a mass of officers travelling to the scene, including the shift sergeant and the police helicopter.

Every time Lauren and Ian passed a landmark, they would let everyone know where they were. As they came up to a roundabout, the lorry did not even slow down; he went straight over the roundabout and carried on. How the trailer did not become detached amazed Ian, Lauren and James. As the lorry slowed slightly, Ian thought this was an opportune time to get in front of it, so he started going around him, on the left in the oncoming lane. The lorry driver saw him trying to get around him and swerved over, forcing Ian towards a ditch at about 45mph. Ian managed to miss the ditch and get his car back onto the road. Now, with the adrenaline really pumping through him, Ian recovered his nerve and continued the pursuit.

Lauren and Ian both advised everyone on the radios that this driver would ram them or run them over if he got the chance. The lorry was picking up speed and was travelling at about 50mph. Lauren tried several times to swing wide to the left to see what was coming and decide if she wanted to try to get in front of him, but he would immediately swing in front of her.

On one of her swings to the left, she saw a patrol car sitting sideways in the road ahead. Ian got on the radio and started yelling for the cop to get out of the way. He told them that this guy would not stop or even slow down. The cop had to gun his patrol car and drive into the ditch to get out of the way. The lorry driver never even let up as he roared past the patrol car, missing it by inches.

The lorry slowed a little as he came up to a crossroad and then turned right, heading towards Otherton.

Then, strangely, the lorry turned towards a residential area. Ian called control and told them that he thought the man was trying to get to his residence. This was the same address that was on the driver's license, which Ian still had. When the lorry made off, Ian was walking back to his car to get his ticket book and do a PNC check. The male's address was quite close to the police station; literally just around the corner from it.

By now, the police helicopter was overhead. Ian and Lauren had been told to drop back further as roads police car had also taken the lead.

The lorry made several turns; it was amazing that it did not hit any cars, as the urban roads were very tight for a large articulated lorry to be travelling along. The lorry then pulled over in front of a house on the right side of the street. All the cops were only a minute behind and pulled up on the other side of the road. Normally they would have run over to the cab and pulled the driver out. For the safety of everyone, they all stood back to see what the lorry driver would do next.

All the cops kept yelling for him to open the door to his lorry, but got no response from him at all. He just sat there, looking at everyone. Finally, the cops, they decided that they would have to approach the cab.

An armed response officer went first with his Taser in his hand and put the red dot from the laser on the driver's upper body. At about this time, the subject's father came out of the house and wanted to know what was going on. James went and grabbed him, pulling him out of possible harm whilst explaining the situation.

Lauren and two other officers approached the cab. The armed response officer moved towards it too. The driver was still just sitting there, looking out, and Lauren could see his hands were empty. They decided to 'rush' the door, and pulled him out of the truck onto the ground. He was handcuffed and put into a police car. Strangely, he did not struggle or resist arrest and was completely compliant without saying a single word.

Once in custody, Ian breathalysed the lorry driver and saw that he was three times over the limit. Lauren and James reflected that they had made a lucky escape, and could have easily been seriously injured. The chase even made both local and national news.

Chapter Four – Having a Fit

James was working with Chris today, as it was common practice for the probationer to work with different cops to see how they all responded and did various aspects of the job. James would have liked to have been working with Lauren, as he was slowly getting quite keen on her.

Chris had been a cop for ten years; he had previously worked on traffic and was qualified to drive, the faster Volvo V70 D5s and BMW 330i's that, every now again, they got to use as area cars. Chris had managed to get the D5 for the shift, so there was an upside to being out with him today. Chris was a very cool and calm cop; James had yet to see him get annoyed or agitated by anything. He just went about his job in a professional manner, although he did prefer working alone and doing his own thing.

James and Chris loaded their kit in the boot, not that there was much room left with the road cones, rope, spade, brush and accident signs already in there. Out on patrol, it was not too long before they pulled a car driver for using a mobile phone whilst driving, and gave the driver a £60 fine and three points on his licence.

Chris watched James fill out a ticket, and gave him some pointers as he progressed through it. James still felt nervous doing tickets, worried he might make a mistake, but Chris was very reassuring and helpful. The man he was dealing with did not look quite so happy. He sat in the back seat of the police car, looking like a sulking four-year-old who had not managed to get his own way.

About an hour into the shift, a call came in via an ambulance of a male in a distressed state who had become difficult to handle, and they feared for his safety. Chris pressed the 999 button and the lights began to flash, with a roar from the Volvo's five-cylinder diesel engine as they accelerated. They were both pushed slightly back into their seats as the car surged forward. The Volvo's engine felt and sounded so much more powerful than the 1.6 TDCi Ford Focus that James was used to being in. It was not that far to the job; they were with the ambulance and its crew within 5 minutes.

Across the road, James could see two paramedics in their green jumpsuits trying to deal with a male. The male looked to be in his fifties and was quite dishevelled in his black tracksuit bottoms and grey polo neck t-shirt. James got out first and went to the male with the paramedics. He was grunting and shouting, "Leave me alone, leave me alone." The paramedic explained the man's brother had called them. He was worried about him because he was a diabetic and did not always take his insulin when he should.

James tried to take the man by the arm and convey him to the ambulance. Initially, he went with James, then halfway across the road, he started to struggle and the paramedics did their best to calm him down. He did calm down a little, but as soon as they got towards the back of the ambulance, he really started to struggle. James and Chris had no choice but to take him to the ground for his own safety. He held the man's arm at the wrist and, with a push from his right palm on the man's shoulder, he went straight down to the ground. The man had the strength of an ox and it took all of their strength to restrain him.

They struggled to get handcuffs on and had to use two pairs. James then lay on top of the man's legs to stop him thrashing about. It looked harsh, but it was the only safe method to control him. After a further few minutes, the man calmed down and James could get up. James noticed there was a smell of excrement, and the paramedic pointed out that James had excrement on his trousers and on the tip of his baton. In the struggle, the tip of James's ASP had somehow gone up the man's bottom. During the course of the diabetic fit, it had caused the man to lose control of his bowels; not a very pleasant sight or smell.

They all managed to get the man into the ambulance and lying down. The male then started to slowly come round. James took the handcuffs off whilst the ambulance crew hooked him up to various monitors.

Chris told James to travel in the ambulance, just in case he kicked off again. The male did look a sorry sight with cuts to his wrists from the cuffs and a graze on his forehead. As he came around, the paramedic asked how he felt, and he seemed more dazed and bemused by being in an ambulance than anything else. He could not remember anything about the diabetic fit he had just had or what had just happened. He just sat up and started talking normally. Chris followed the ambulance to the hospital. On arrival, James went to the toilet to try and clean himself up a bit, as Chris had told him he was not getting in his police car smelling like he did!

Back at the police station, Chris went into the parade room to pass on his "war story" whilst James got a clean t-shirt and trousers on.

In the parade room, Chris said, "I really did get James in the shit this time."

Chris then proceeded to tell the rest of the story, with laughs and smiles from the cops in the room.

On his way back to the parade room, James bumped into Lauren, who was off to the kitchen to cook her tea. Lauren's definition of cooked meant zapped in the microwave for a few minutes. She seemed quite concerned about how he was, making sure he had cleaned all his kit properly. Had he bagged the soiled kit up and put it in the special bin to be destroyed? She sounded more like his mum than his tutor. James could not help but gaze into her blue eyes that drew him in.

Back out on patrol, Chris was telling James his life story. Chris certainly had a lot of life experience, having been a teacher for a short period before becoming a police officer. He laughed that there was actually more paperwork in the police than he had ever had as a teacher, even with all the marking and student reports he had to write. The best part of being a teacher was the long holidays, although they were very much needed after a busy term. The holidays were great if you had a family. Chris had two teenage boys and would often tell everyone who cared to listen, about their antics.

However, Chris did not find teaching active enough. He loved the teaching element, but not all the extras you were expected to do and the weekends spent marking. So much red tape, even more than the police service, made him decide on a career change. Most of the time, when you finished your shift with the police, you could go home and that was the end of it. On the odd occasion, you may have to pop in to get some urgent paperwork completed on a day off, or get stuck on duty. You would at least get paid overtime after the "golden hour" due to a serious incident or needing to complete a job.

Chris' life story was soon interrupted by a call to go to a job. This time, the call was to an RTC; a car was reported to be upside down in a ditch. Both Chris and James thought this might well be serious. No other cars were involved, thankfully. Chris and James quickly made their way to the scene. On arrival, fire and ambulance were already there. Chris decided straight away that the best thing to do was block the road off, and then ask another unit to go and close the road at the roundabout.

James went over to the car in the ditch and, sure enough, it was upside down on its roof. The rear window was smashed, as were a couple of the side windows. One front wheel was buckled and the car was in quite a sorry state. The badge on the back read 416i; James instantly knew it was a Rover 400.

Amazingly, the man driving the car had managed to drag himself out. He had a few injuries, but nothing major and was very lucky. Before he was taken away, Chris went and breathalysed him, which came back as a negative result. According to a witness, the car had swerved for some reason and the driver had over-compensated and clipped the curb, which in turn had caused the car to come off the road and flip into the air before landing on its roof in the ditch. He had made a lucky escape.

With fire and ambulance having left the scene and witness details taken, all Chris and James could do was wait for the recovery vehicle. Recovery would now be a little more difficult as it was starting to rain. One impatient driver had already tried to go around the stationary police car with its lights flashing. The driver ended up with a telling off from Chris and his details being taken.

The recovery truck arrived within half an hour of James requesting it. The car was winched out of the ditch before being turned back over and lifted onto the back of the recovery truck. The whole car was covered in large dents, its metallic red paintwork split like an open wound in several areas. It did look in a sorry state and was more than likely a write-off due to its age.

With the car recovered, the road could be re-opened and Chris and James could make their way to the hospital to check on the driver and also find out if any next of kin needed informing. This was their second trip of the shift to the local hospital.

At the hospital, Chris went to check with the doctor what the actual injuries were for the accident card. He had been lucky with only a dislocated collar bone, some cuts and bruises to his head, and severe bruising to his leg. X-rays would give a better idea of any other injuries, but this was enough for Chris. to be able to fill out the accident card. Both Chris and James wondered if the man had been on his mobile phone or fiddling with the stereo at the time, causing him to swerve.

The man was actually on his way home after visiting his children and ex-wife. The man just wanted the friend he was lodging with notifying of the accident, which Chris and James said they would do on their way back to the nick to get the night's paperwork done before going off duty.

CHAPTER FIVE - NIGHT OUT

James was looking forward to his night out with the shift and some from Rota 2, along with a few specials and police community support officers, after four months of being a cop. They were all due to meet in a local pub, The Brazen, which was one of those new trendy pubs which had only recently opened just around the corner from the police station. A few were already in the bar when James arrived; a couple of specials, Jayne and Reece, were chatting at the bar. James could hear Ian talking to what looked like a blonde-haired woman with long hair in the corner.

As James approached, the blonde-haired woman turned around and said, "Hello James. Glad you could make it."

His heart skipped a beat; he was taken aback by the beautiful woman standing in front of him. Lauren looked very different out of uniform with her hair down and in full make-up.

She looked every bit like Holly Valance; her hair was long and straight, makeup perfectly done, and she wore a slightly fitted, above-the-knee red dress that accentuated her curves. She looked even taller than normal in her big heels, like those worn by Victoria Beckham, and black opaque tights finished off the outfit.

James just replied, "Errr, hello," as he was still spellbound by how good Lauren looked.

"Can I get anyone a drink?" James then asked, just so it did not look like he was staring at Lauren.

"If you are buying, James, make mine a glass of wine," Lauren said with a cheeky smile.

"Get me a bottle of Becks," replied Ian.

The night had started well, and everyone got on with the usual shop talk and comparing "war stories." From The Brazen, everyone piled into a couple of taxis and headed into the city centre. A couple of bars later, everyone was more than a little merry.

By now, the women were getting ready for a dance. "Club time. Any ideas?" After blank looks from the men, the women ended up deciding for them and gently pushed them towards the Lizard Lounge. The Lizard Lounge was quite a trendy niche club on the edge of the city centre.

Lauren approached James in a slightly drunk manner; she was interested to learn more about him. They had spent a long time next to each other, chatting about all sorts, but both had been quite guarded on what they would talk about. She wanted to know a little more about James the person, especially the type of women he went for, without being too obvious.

They compared notes on family and friends, then Lauren just came out with it in a slightly drunken slur: "Who is the lady in your life then?"

James was a little taken aback and just said, "No one. Been single for the past year."

Lauren said, "Oh dear, what happened? I am surprised a nice bloke like you is single. What is your story then, James?"

James had planned to move in with his ex, Christina and had even thought about marrying her. That sadly had all fallen apart when

58

Christina had an affair with a work colleague. She had begged James for forgiveness, but James felt that the trust they had was gone and the hurt was too great. His heart had been ripped out and stamped on. He had not seen or spoken to her for nine months, and was happy to throw himself into his new job and make a fresh start.

Lauren listened intently, and her eyes twinkled at him. He knew she was quite drunk but felt there was something between them. Lauren grabbed James' hand and pulled him onto the dance floor, and they were dancing closely. Like with Christina, James could feel his heart racing and he started to get a dry mouth. James and Lauren's eyes met and they were drawn to each other. Then they both looked away as if to try to hide their attraction. Finally, their lips touched; her soft, warm lips sent a shiver down James's spine. James placed his arm around Lauren's slender waist. James was quite taken aback; they kissed for a while, then all of a sudden. Lauren pulled back.

"I am so sorry, James. That should never have happened. You're a great lad but, err." James stood staring at Lauren for a few moments and, unlike his usual quiet self, he said, "I know, I know. Better not go any further."

James was shocked by his own sensible words and, by the look on her face, so was Lauren. She walked off the dance floor, leaving James standing there unsure, of what to do next. Lauren tried to act as if nothing had happened and James just followed her lead, not wanting to look stupid either. Lauren was worried that she had crossed the line with her student, and did not want feelings to get in the way of professionalism. James was her student, a student she had developed feelings for. Feelings that had just crept up on her, and feelings that she should really supress.

Chapter Six – Drugs Raid

After his four rest days, James was back on duty wondering how things would be between him and Lauren. The day after the night out, he had had a really big hangover and realised the reason he did not go out drinking very often, besides the astronomical cost.

He had not spoken to or texted Lauren since the night out, but had been surprised that she just behaved as though nothing had happened. He had hoped, she maybe would want to take things further or tell James what a great kisser he was. Nevertheless, she just said and did nothing; in many ways, this was worse than just being ignored. Rumours were rife, but then that was normal. Lauren knew that after a few days they would blow over.

James took Lauren's lead and behaved as if nothing had happened as well. Although, deep down, he wished something had; he had grown fond of Lauren as he had got to know her better. She was 25 to his 23 and had 6 years' service already under her belt. She joined as soon as she could, although it had taken her three attempts to get in. She was well respected by all the cops and was almost like a mother hen to many of the cops and PCSOs.

Today, Lauren had gotten James assigned to a warrant on a suspected cannabis factory with the Neighbourhood Police Team. Lauren thought it might be a good experience, as well as a chance to get to know the NPT team better. He had to get in for a briefing at five, ready for the warrant being executed at six. In the briefing room today was a collection of two beat managers, 3 PCSOs and a special who was obviously very keen to turn in at six in the morning. James had spoken to all of them over the past few weeks, although nothing more than a hello and goodbye or a few quick words at various jobs they had attended together. Everyone looked a little bleary-eyed; most of them usually worked shifts ranging from seven until one in the morning. James, however, did not feel too tired, even though he had been up since four.

The warrant was on a house only about a mile from the police station. It was a 1940s terrace that had been rented; intelligence had come in that it was being used to grow cannabis plants. Quite a bit of safety information was given out as, at previous raids on other properties, they had found the door handles had been made live with mains electricity or a strip of nails on window ledges or just inside doors.

They all piled into a police van followed by the NPT sergeant and a beat manager in a police car behind. The property was not that far away, and they pulled up the van further down the road to make sure the occupants of the property were not alerted to their presence.

One of the beat managers was in riot gear and carried the "Enforcer," which was used to break doors down. The Enforcer was basically a red metal ram with two handles. The property was occupied by two people; according to intelligence, one of them was a known local criminal, and the other occupant had no previous record on PNC.

James and the others stood back, away from the door, as the beat manager moved forward. It was an old wooden door stained in an oak colour, which was peeling after years of being battled by the elements. It still took several heavy blows with the enforcer to bash the door open. Then everyone piled in. James was told to stay at the rear in case they made a run for it out the back door or window. The beat managers went straight up the stairs to check for the occupants; the special and the sergeant went straight into the living room. In unison, the beat managers shouted down to say they had both occupants handcuffed and were bringing them downstairs.

James felt a little lost, not knowing what to do, so he stood at the bottom of the stairs to help the two occupants down, followed by the beat managers.

Everyone was now in his or her assigned room and checking for any signs of drugs, when the special shouted out.

"Got something... Found some cannabis plants and hydroponics equipment in the bathroom."

One beat manager, who was now the exhibits officer, shouted up.

"Make a note of everything and let me know before dismantling any of it."

By now, James was in the kitchen emptying everything out of the cupboards. The important part of a search was doing it in a logical order so nothing was missed.

In one cupboard that housed the boiler, he did find a couple of small bags of cannabis and passed these onto the exhibits officer. This meant he would need to do a seizure statement when back at the station.

Everyone was at the house for about two hours, searching every nook and cranny. Both the men inside the house were arrested for "Intent to supply a controlled substance;" even though it looked and smelt like cannabis, it was referred to as green vegetable matter until a test had proven otherwise.

As James walked out of the house, a woman came up to him and asked what was going on. She also asked James his name, and then announced that she lived next door, but worked for the local newspaper.

She started firing questions at James. Unsure of what to say, he just went bright red and said, "Err," in his usual manner.

Luckily, the beat sergeant came out and said to the reporter,

"Can you leave my officers alone? There is nothing going on, and if we have anything to say, it will be via the press office."

The reporter looked a little stunned and was lost for words.

"But…" she said.

The sergeant said, "But nothing. Kindly leave us and let us get on with our job."

"Wow." thought James at the way the reporter had been handled. He really must get more assertive when dealing with people. Lauren had told him that he was too polite at times and needed to be more business-like, otherwise people would take advantage.

Back at the station, James wrote up his seizure statement with help from a beat manager, who had sent him a recent statement he had done.

"I am a Police Constable 3468 SOWMAN of Hampshire Police, currently stationed at Otherton.

I was on duty in full uniform on 17th December 2010 at 06:30 when I attended 79 SWINEY Road, Otherton, to assist other officers in the execution of a search warrant as part of an ongoing investigation. Whilst at the address, I seized the following items.

I seized two bags containing green vegetable matter from a kitchen cupboard that housed the boiler. These are now known as JS/1.

I subsequently handed these exhibits to PC557 NEEDHAM, the exhibits' officer."

When everyone was finished, the Beat managers took orders for a breakfast cob from the sandwich shop on the high street.

James had enjoyed doing the warrant and he was to stay with the beat team for the rest of the shift. This was so James could see what they did. He had already spent a week in custody learning all about booking prisoners in and dealing with a whole variety of people. There had been a man who had spread excrement on the cell walls in protest at his arrest. A couple of others had threatened to commit suicide and had to be closely watched all the time via CCTV. James really did get to see people at their worst while working in custody.

It had been a long day and just before James was due to get off, they got a call to say the local primary school had been broken into. James was with the beat manager for the area in which the school was located. They raced to the scene and, burglary being a current priority, the dogs and helicopter were called in.

A ground unit was already at the scene, so James and the beat manager decided to wait just around the corner. They both got out of the car and made their way down some alleyways towards the school. The helicopter was overhead by now, but struggling to locate anyone in the bushes and trees that surrounded the school.

Movement, had been seen not too far from where James was searching, and he proceeded to climb over a rather large wall. Just has he got down, the dog man shouted,

"GET OUT, I AM GOING TO LET THE DOG IN"

James leapt back over the wall. The dog made its way in and within a few seconds was barking its head off. They had found one of the burglars hiding in the undergrowth; the police helicopter had failed to see it, but the dog had no problem. Cops inside the school found the other person - another teenage male - so a nice result all round.

Meanwhile, the police helicopter had offered to go and search for a suspicious group seen walking down the road about two miles away. On arrival, the police helicopter found the group to be carol singers as they watched them go from door to door, carol singing.

The beat manager laughed and said, "Dog one, helicopter nil." This made James laugh, especially after watching "Chopper Coppers" and such like, when the helicopter always got their 'man.' Well, nearly always...

CHAPTER SEVEN – YOU'RE NEVER OFF DUTY

Typical first day off - James woke up early and could not get back to sleep. It was only 7am and James pulled the curtains open to watch everyone else hurry themselves off to work. It was not that long ago that James was doing the same. He thought back to when he was at university and had thought about joining the army. He was unsure, so his dad had told him to go join the Territorial Army. He spent five years in the TA. It had been a good way to earn money whilst at university. It also gave him a reason to keep fit, as he had to pass an annual fitness test. James was due to be deployed to Afghanistan for a 6 month tour before he passed all his tests and was accepted into the police. This meant his police training course would start whilst he was deployed. James really wanted to go, but his parents were not quite so happy with the thought that their son could be maimed or killed like so many other soldiers. With the demands of training, James made the decision to quit the TA with the thought that he may go back in a couple of years.

He made some good friends in the TA; some he had met on his basic training and during his officer training, which he had failed first time round. In basic training, it was easy to just listen and do as you are told. If you are shouted at, just take it on the chin, a corporal from his squadron had told him. The training was designed to put you under pressure to weed out those that may crack under the stress of battle.

One day, during an officer inspection, James had his boots thrown out of the window for having a bit of fluff on them. Two weeks later,

James passed out as a qualified soldier and felt a real sense of achievement.

After two years, his Officer Commanding asked him if he fancied going through officer selection and training. James decided to give it a go. He failed his first selection board, who told him to come back in six months. He did, and then passed. After that it was various other smaller courses he had to pass, before spending three weeks at the Royal Military Academy, Sandhurst, for his commissioning course. The place itself made James feel nervous, and he did struggle on the course from day one, falling apart when giving orders. James failed the course the first time, but went back a year later and passed out as a 2nd Lieutenant.

After finishing his degree in civil engineering, James had decided it was not the career for him. Struggling to find a job, he got a position at a call centre. He hated being treated like a battery hen, reading scripts and being told off if he deviated from them. After two weeks, James just walked out and said goodbye after getting a call offering him a job selling cars.

Selling cars was not as easy as it sounded. It was rare he got a weekend off. It was long hours, 9-7, and six days a week. James really enjoyed the job initially; he got a nice, newish Vauxhall Astra to drive around in, and £20 worth of fuel a week. The buzz of making a sale was great, but this was linked with hours of boredom and drinking tea or chasing customers. Even though he was well educated with a degree, people would treat him as if he were stupid just because he sold cars.

When he read in the paper that the local police force was recruiting, he thought he would give it a go. Knowing the chances of getting in were very slim, he got a couple of good books, which helped a little. The application form on its own was a mammoth task, but he found that the TA and uni had given him some good examples for the so-called "core competencies." He had to write examples of times when he had shown or undertook team working, respect for diversity, prioritising, resilience, conflict resolution and problem solving. He spent hours filling in the application form in his best handwriting, making sure he did not make a mistake. After all, over 60% of people do not get past the application stage. All the effort must have worked as he got through to the next stage at the assessment centre, receiving a letter after two months congratulating him.

The assessment centre was five hours of hell. There were English and maths tests, followed by a leisure centre scenario in which he had to play the customer manager and deal with various customer issues. The customers were all played by actors and seemed very real. James actually enjoyed the day; he tried to remember what he had read in the various books he had bought and took all the tips on board. James hated tests and almost felt sick as he walked into his first assessment. He did well again to pass first time with a good overall grade. Then there was just the final interview, before he had to wait for his intake date and the start of his training.

James got ready and realised he had an empty fridge so needed to go shopping; he was amazed how busy a supermarket could be on a weekday morning. He forgot the golden rule of "never go shopping on an empty stomach," as you end up buying stuff you do not really need. With his trolley half full, feeling quite pleased with the various offers he had been able to get, he went towards the checkout.

Out of the corner of his eye, he spotted a male in his twenties looking a bit shifty, constantly looking left and then right as he scurried towards the door. He was too far off to see his face as it was hidden by a hoody. As he passed a shelf, near to the exit, he picked something up, although it was too far away to see. James thought, "Great." Even on his day off, he wanted to avoid police work, but felt duty-bound to do something. Leaving his trolley, he quickly made his way towards the exit to find the nearest security guard.

As he got closer, he could see the security guard was already with the male and he could hear raised voices. The security guard was attempting to get the chap back into the store, but he was having none of it, shouting,

"Get off, get off."

James moved quickly and went to the security guard's aid, saying, "Need a hand? I am an off-duty police officer." James thought it sounded rather lame, but he could tell the security guard was grateful for the extra help.

James could tell the male they were grappling with was drunk just from the strong smell of alcohol on his breath. They moved the man back into the store and managed to calm him down. When he lifted his head up, James instantly recognised him from a disturbance they had attended in the park last week. Lauren had been great at talking him round, and he had even allowed them to take him back to the homeless shelter.

His name was Richard Blake. He was in his twenties and used to work as a computer programmer for a big software company nearby. He was married with two kids, but the death of his mother had turned him to alcohol and his whole life had spiralled out of control. He had already been in prison for threatening a police officer with a knife and violent disorder. Richard was also banned from several shops and supermarkets for shoplifting. A very sad case; his kids had lost a dad and his wife a husband; all due to alcohol.

Richard started to get agitated again, saying,

"I want to go. Let me go, or I will stab you."

James just said, "Hi, Richard. Remember me? I took you back to your refuge last week."

Richard looked up, slightly puzzled, but did seem to recognise James and calmed down slightly.

Richard said to James, "Please can I just go? I have not done anything."

James said, "We will get everything sorted mate, don't worry." James did not want to upset him further by saying he would be arrested when the cavalry arrived.

James could hear the siren before he could see the flashing blue lights of a police car as it weaved its way through the quite full car park and came to a stop outside the front of the supermarket. Out jumped PC Steve Bainbridge and PC Adams, both from James's police station on Rota 4.

"Hey James," PC Steve Bainbridge said.

James looked up and said "Hiya" as he continued to hold Richard down. PC Bainbridge then applied the handcuffs so that he and James could pick Richard up. PC Adams had already gone to talk to the security guard, who by now was standing up and leaving James and

Steve to it. The security guard then explained what he had seen and heard, saying it should all be on CCTV.

PC Adams said, "Great. If you can get that sorted for me and write a statement... Oh, and what was the cost of the items he stole?"

Bainbridge and Adams took Richard to the police car and off to custody. James went back to his abandoned trolley and finally went through the checkout.

James had promised to pop into his mum and dad's for tea, having not seen them for two weeks due to his shifts and his mum and dad's rather hectic social life. His dad just worked part-time after taking early redundancy from his teaching job. His mum had been a financial advisor, but got fed up with the job and various changes at the bank she worked for. She made the decision to retire completely and took early retirement when they offered it.

James was close to his mum, dad and sister. His sister was three years younger than James was. She had just finished university, but was still living at home. She had got a part-time job and had been able to increase her hours whilst she tried to find something better, but really did not enjoy having to move back home after three years of living away.

It was only three years ago that James' dad, John had found out he was adopted, after someone had told him at the funeral of his adopted mother. James' dad had always had an inkling he was adopted, but his adopted mother had never divulged this to him. He was adopted not long after his adopted mother's son died after being scolded by a pan of boiling water.

This had led James' dad, John to try to search for his actual parents after 59 years. He had heard the name Fewson spoken about and got in contact with an aunt, who lived on the Isle of Wight. She knew very little, other than he was adopted and had been picked up from Sheffield not long after he was born, and the name Starky and Wallis were on the adoption papers. His father had died in the Second World War, going down with his ship. With this information, John contacted the services to see if they had any record of a Fewson.

He waited and waited, and got nothing back. Then, by chance, he decided to get in contact with the Merchant Navy, and they proved to be a lot more efficient. After two weeks, he got a reply that said his father, third Officer Fewson Wallis, had died in 1941 when his ship, the "Chinese Prince," had been torpedoed by U-552, commandeered by Eric Topp. Out of a crew of 65, only 19 had survived.

John then got in contact with his aunt in the Isle of Wight and passed on the information. She had meanwhile found a letter that talked about a family in Preston.

As John searched, he found no record of anyone by the name "Fewson Starky" in Preston Lancashire. He realised there was another Preston just outside of Hull. Armed with the information, John and his wife set off to Hull and then to Preston for the day. Not sure where to look, they went to the church to see if there were any records and did actually find a plaque with Fewson's name on it.

John had a love of pies, and by chance, they went past a butcher's shop that sold amazing pies. He decided to stop and get one for tea. When in the shop, John asked the butcher if he knew a family called Starky or Wallis living in the area, to which he replied, "Oh yes, there is a Norman Starkey, who lives just round the corner from here." John made his way to the house and rang the doorbell, and an old gentleman came to the door. John was not really sure what to say so explained that he was adopted, and one parent was Wallace and the other Starky. The man had a blank look on his face when his wife came to the door and seemed to know exactly what he was talking about.

It seemed that James' grandfather had gone down with his ship trying to save his crew - a true hero. He was on his way home to marry James' grandmother Peggy, who was pregnant with James' dad at the time. In 1941, being born out of wedlock was not the done thing, so Peggy's family refused to help. Encouraged by the ACF, John was put up for adoption. Peggy, quite grief stricken, had later met a Canadian soldier and emigrated to Canada at the end of the war. She was still living out there with three daughters. The sisters were excited to have a new half-brother, but Peggy did not want to make contact. Maybe she was embarrassed, or maybe it was just too painful?

James had always thought what an amazing story it was, and now he had a completely new family up in Hull, although he did not see them very often.

"Hi mum,"James said, as he gave his mum a kiss on the cheek and walked in. James and his mum had always got on well, although not without the odd argument or two over the years. James loved his mum's cooking and it was nice to not be eating on his own, as was normal on his days off.

Halfway through his meal, he got a text from Lauren asking if they could meet up for a drink. James thought nothing of it other than that it must be a social get together; things had been a little tense since the infamous 'kiss' a couple of months ago. James replied, "Yep, fine. Meet at the Griffins Head at 8pm?"

"James, what are you doing on that phone at the tea table?" asked James' mum in a slightly off tone.

"Err, just replying to Lauren. Going to meet her later." James replied.

James' mum just raised her eyebrows and said nothing more.

After tea, James sat down with his mum and dad for a cup of tea and a good chat about what he had been up to. He forgot the time, and when he realised it was nearly 8pm, he had to make a rush for the door.

His mum was very good at reading James, and said,

"Meeting a lady friend then, James? You're keeping this one quiet."

"Err, yes it is a woman. Just a friend from work," James replied, blushing ever so slightly.

James made it to the pub for about five past eight, and thankfully Lauren was just pulling into the car par. James parked his car next to hers.

They both got out almost simultaneously. As ever, Lauren looked beautiful; her hair and make-up had been done immaculately, and she had the nicest smelling perfume on. Her well-toned legs were in a pair of skinny jeans coupled with a top and thick belt. Her high-heeled knee-high boots made a tapping sound as they walked across the car park.

James' heart started to flutter yet again, the first time since they had kissed on the dance floor. They had worked together, but kept things very professional, and neither had said a word about the kiss, preferring to keep with friendly banter and shop talk. However, both knew things were not the same.

The pub was an old-fashioned traditional one with beams running across the roof. Hung on the walls were black-and-white pictures of the area a hundred years ago.

James bought the first round of drinks and they sat down next to the fire, which was crackling away.

James still thought Lauren had the most amazing eyes. Personally, he had never seen the big deal about blue eyes. Probably because most blue eyes were a pale, washed-out kind of blue, but not Lauren's. They were the bluest blue eyes he had ever seen. They really made her face light up and were so expressive.

Snapping out of an almost trance-like spell, James realised he was staring dumbfounded. He had not even answered her. His eyes left hers and darted around the pub.

"You have really lovely eyes."

James thought it sounded so corny, but Lauren just smiled and said, "Yeah... You always make me laugh."

He moved his chair away from the fire as his back was getting a little too hot. Lauren aimed a polite smile at him.

"What have you been up to?"

James told Lauren about the shoplifter he had helped apprehend earlier on in the day.

"You been up to anything exciting?" asked James.

"I'm a bit of a writer sometimes. Well, most of the time actually. It is hard for me to drag myself away from the computer on my days off. If I didn't pace myself, I'd be at it twenty-four seven. Managed to tear myself away this afternoon for a meet up with Tracy."

"You never told me you wrote. What do you write? Cookery books?" James laughed.

"I'll have you know I have written and published two books! Although someone I do not get on with has got wind of it and decided it would be funny to leave a load of one star reviews saying how bad the book was. I think they are just jealous. It's a shame that people feel the need to have a go at your hard work. I am hardly a bestselling novelist or the world's greatest writer."

Lauren smiled and those blue eyes suddenly widened, and she shook her head, obviously chagrined. "Would you listen to me? Apparently, I don't talk to my friends often enough."

James smiled. "That's such a shame. People can get worked up and jealous over the smallest things. I've seen that for myself just going to domestics. My friends say the same. I totally understand now, being a cop; not the best of jobs for a decent social life. The strange and varied hours, and then for some reason, as soon as anyone you do meet realises you are a cop, they back off."

Both James and Lauren had started to open up a bit more, especially Lauren, who chatted away about her life before the police. James listened intently as this was the first time she had opened up. Lauren was still a bit guarded about herself, not wanting to let too much out all at once. She had been hurt before, and saying too much had been the downfall in all of her relationships. James cracked another joke and Lauren laughed again, her eyes sparkling. She took James' hand and said,

"That kiss we had did mean something to me. I am really fond of you. I was just… worried about what everyone would say and did not want to be unprofessional. I would like to see you more, if that's ok?"

James' eyes now widened; he was a bit taken aback, and his heart started to race. Was it a trick question, or was that an offer from Lauren of something more?

"I would like that very much," said James, still a bit taken aback. He had it all planned on what he intended to say and now, Lauren had taken the words out of his mouth. Lauren then continued with a remark that deflated James very slightly.

"The thing is, it does need to be kept quiet. It will cause all sorts of issues and gossip at work," said Lauren.

James felt a bit sad that he could not share his happiness with others, but also felt Lauren was holding something back from him.

The rest of the night they sat close to each other, chatting away and laughing, mainly at James' rather bad jokes such as, "Did you hear about the car thief in the multi-story car park? It was crime on every level!"

James had decided not to drink as he could not be bothered with a taxi home. Lauren, in contrast, had had several glasses of wine and by now was rather tipsy. They stayed in the pub until closing time, and then James took Lauren home and helped her inside. She made a drink and sat down on the sofa. Lauren leant over and initiated a kiss; the kiss became a long, lingering one as James wrapped his arms around Lauren. This time, Lauren did not pull away. She was enjoying James' warm embrace and passionate kiss. Lauren removed James's shirt and James returned the favour by removing Lauren's top.

Their bodies slapped together, mouths still locked as his groans joined hers.

Much later, after moving upstairs, with no duvet left on the bed, Lauren's eyes drifted closed. Beyond exhaustion, James recovered the duvet, drew it over her body and then kissed her forehead as he settled into sleep beside her.

CHAPTER EIGHT – STOLEN TRACTOR

Time for another night shift, and before anyone had time to sit down, an immediate call came in of a drunk driver on the A27 weaving across the road. The afternoon shift was all tied up, which meant Rota 2 had to turn out. Everyone made a quick exit, picking up the first set of car keys they could find on the key board before moving quickly to the cars. Ian and Chris got off first, with blue lights flashing as they made their way through the front gate like a scalded cat.

James and Lauren jumped in and started the police car up before making their way out of the station, not far behind Ian and Chris. It only took a couple of minutes for Ian to catch up with the drunk driver. Even with his blues and twos on, the driver failed to stop so Ian had to call in the traffic police who had cars that were allowed to pursue; all Ian could do was follow at a safe distance whilst Chris gave a running commentary.

The drunk driver was in a very nice Audi A4 convertible, and had already managed to blow a front tyre out. Then, at the next roundabout, he hit the curb and took the second front tyre out. Chris passed the registration number and found the car had not been reported stolen. With both tyres now blown, the car began to slow down, and sparks flew off the front wheels as the car drove on its alloy wheel rims.

The traffic cars announced they were only a few minutes away, and Lauren and James were now behind Ian and Chris as they followed. Then, without warning, the car pulled over into a layby and came to a stop. Ian jumped out, followed by Chris, and ran to the driver's door.

Chris opened it whilst Ian pulled the driver out. He could barely stand and just fell to the floor. The driver looked to be in his 30s and was wearing a smart suit, as if he had just come from work. James and Lauren rushed in to help and got the driver stood up. Once stood up, Lauren retrieved the car keys, secured the car and passed the keys to Chris.

The driver then said in a very slurred tone, "Leave me alone, I Just wanna go home."

James helped Ian get the driver handcuffed and in the back of his police car; the man was still ranting and swearing. Ian asked if he would provide a sample of breath, to which he refused on several occasions by saying, "Fuck off." Ian gave up and asked Chris to sit next him in the rear of the car, ready to make their way to custody. If he refused to provide a sample of breath in custody, he would be charged with failing to provide and get a 12 to 18 month driving ban.

Lauren felt it was going to be "one of those nights," when they would be rushing from one job to another. The minute Ian and Chris had driven off to custody, another call came in for an immediate response to a domestic in one of the villages that fell into E Division, but all their cops were tied up and Lauren and James were the nearest resource.

It took a good 10 minutes to get to the house. On arrival, the front door was open, and James and Lauren made their way into the front room. Inside were two women and two children. One of the women was crying with a blood stained t-shirt and bright-red nose, as if she had been punched. She told Lauren and James that her ex-boyfriend had come round. He was also the father of the two children and had come round to see them. She had let him in and after an hour, they got into what was initially just verbal argument, but it had escalated. He had then smashed the LCD TV, which now had a giant crack across it, before punching Jenny in the face.

In the corner of the room sat the quite large black Samsung LCD TV, looking quite sorry for itself with a large crack in the top left hand corner of the screen.

This was not the first time Jenny had been hit by Steve. When Lauren had done a check for previous incidents at the property, control had said there had been four other domestic incidents there. This though was the first involving violence. Steve was known to the police, and even had markers for being violent and assaulting police whenever he had been drinking.

Steve had left about 10 minutes ago; it was thought he had headed back to his parents' address. Lauren spent another few minutes getting basic details before she said to Jenny,

"We will go and see if we can find Steve and arrest him, then we will come back to take a statement and fill out the domestic pack."

Lauren and James jumped into the police car and did a search of the area, but to no avail. Luckily they had Steve's parents address from previous incidents, so they made their way there. Steve's parents were helpful and used to his bad behaviour when he had been drinking. Sadly, he was not there, but they said they would ring the police as and when he came home.

James and Lauren went back to Jenny's to take a statement and do all the other necessary paperwork. After they had been there an hour, control radioed through.

"Steve's parents have rung to say he has turned up back home."

With this, Lauren sped up the pace and informed Jenny that they knew where Steve was and would go and arrest him for ABH (Actual Bodily Harm). Laura seemed semi-happy with this; it was obvious she still had feelings for him, but hated the way he treated her.

Lauren and James went back to the property. Chris and Ian had offered to come as back-up due to the violent markers Steve had against his name. Lauren and James knocked at the door, and Steve's mother answered.

"Hiya, come on in. He has gone to bed to sleep it off."

Lauren let James go first to see how he would handle it. James knocked on the door and walked in. The smell of stale beer was what hit James first, which was in total contrast to the very neat and tidy bedroom. Steve was already awake and sat up in bed, not surprised to see the police judging by the look on his face.

James said in a soft tone, "Alright mate, sorry to wake you, but you need to come with us. I am sure you know what it is about. Better get some clothes on so we can take you in."

To James' surprise, he just got out of bed, half-asleep and still slightly drunk. He got dressed, whilst trying to explain what had happened. He came almost too quietly, and James was surprised at how nice he was; surely this could not be the same person with markers against him for violence and police assault?

Lauren cancelled, Chris and Ian with Steve being compliant; he even had no issues with being handcuffed, although did not like being handcuffed to the rear and moaned a little all the way to custody. The handcuffs were not quite the pink fluffy ones from Ann Summers, and even during training, James had gone home with enough marks around his wrists to look as if he had been self-harming.

Once in the car, James cautioned Steve and did it faultlessly for the first time.

"I am arresting you on suspicion of ABH; you do not have to say anything, but it may harm your defence if you do not mention when questioned something which you later rely on in court. Anything you do say may be given in evidence."

Custody had the usual smell - a mixture of alcohol, disinfectant and sick that hit them as they walked through the door and made their way to the booking-in desk. Steve was still being really well-behaved and was very grateful to have the handcuffs removed. James asked Steve to empty his pockets whilst the custody sergeant took his details and got him booked in.

James offered to take him to the cells as the custody officers were busy with another prisoner who was shouting and screaming. With that done, Lauren and James were free to leave and go back to the station to complete all the paperwork.

On the way back ,they made plans for what to do on their days off. James suggested going to London for the day, and Lauren thought going somewhere shopping, sounded like a nice idea. Just as they were almost halfway back to the station, the next call came in over the radio.

"Alpha Romeo 377."

"Go ahead," replied Lauren.

"Can you attend an immediate report of a tractor having been abandoned on the side of the A3 next to Cramford House? One runner, but no description."

Lauren sighed and said, "Show us travelling"

Ian and James were still sorting out a fight outside a takeaway so there was nobody else available.

"Guess the paperwork will have to wait," said Lauren, as she switched on the blue lights and made swift progress to the scene. On arrival, they spotted an old yellow tractor that was on the grass verge at the side of the road, with the back end sticking out into the road. A front and rear tyre had partially come off. It was an old Forden tractor. James thought, "What a strange vehicle to take for a joy ride."

Plant equipment theft was something James had been to before, being in a more rural area. Plant equipment is quite easy to steal, with very few fitted with immobilisers, deadlocks or tracking devices. Very few people, including police officers, knew the location of the VIN plates. Most plant was stolen between 8pm and 5am and then put onto the back of a trailer, before it was either broken up for parts or exported to continental Europe, from the Balkans to Greece or Poland through to Russia. Some plant equipment would also find its way to the Middle East via shipping containers.

The police dog had been called, so James and Lauren waited in the car to make it easier for the dog to pick up the scent without them contaminating the scene. The dog found a trail, but it went cold behind some farm buildings, and with it being dark, there was very little hope of finding the offender. Having no registration, it was hard to find out who owned the tractor. Being in an unsafe position meant it needed to be recovered. Thankfully, the recovery truck only took half an hour to get there.

The minute the recovery truck pulled away, yet another job came in. This was a report via ambulance of a man who had attempted to kill himself.

On arrival, it was as if nothing had happened; the ambulance had gone and all there was to see was a tearful teenager at the front door of the house. James and Lauren got out and James went to speak to the boy. Still in tears, the boy took them to the back garden where Chris and Ian were already searching the scene.

Ian said, "Have a look in the shed."

The shed was covered in blood; most of it was at the bottom of a large mirror and was very thick and bright red. The boy's father had tried to take his own life by putting a cordless electric drill into his head and then drilling into the side of his skull. A yellow cordless drill covered in blood stains lay in the pool of blood. .

The man was still alive and conscious and was on his way to hospital. The ambulance crew would remain unsure of the extent of his injuries or whether any brain damage had occurred until he had been checked over and had a brain scan. The scene made James feel sick and his thoughts went to the man's son who was standing alone in the garden, worried sick about his father.

Ian and Chris were going to stay at the scene and wait for CSI, which meant Lauren and James were no longer needed.

Finally, Lauren and James could go back to the station to finish off paperwork and get some much-needed tea; they had not stopped for the past seven hours.

CHAPTER NINE – ICE SKATING

Somehow, Lauren had managed to convince James to go ice-skating on one of their days off. James had persuaded Lauren to go paintballing a couple of weeks ago, so now it was Lauren's turn to dictate what they did. James had ice-skated as a 16-year old, going down to the ice rink on Saturday afternoons to skate and meet girls. When they arrived, James had to go to the skate hire to get some skates. Lauren used to do figure skating as a teenager and still had her slightly worn-looking white ice skates.

The peppy organ music took James back to when he was a teenager. He could see that the rink was already crowded, with numerous skaters of all ages sliding around at differing speeds. He picked up the rental skates and found a spot on the bench at the edge of the ice. As he laced up his skates, he heard a whistle blow. At the far end of the rink, he saw two skaters shouting at each other - one a woman with a whistle around her neck, the other a man who stood three or more inches taller than her. James could tell she was winning the argument; her voice was loud and angry above the din of music, skater conversations and the slice noise of the multitude of skate blades. From her gestures, he surmised, she was telling him to slow down or she would throw him out.

James would not have to worry about breaking her speed rules. It was years since he last skated and he knew he would end up on his bottom at least once. James and Lauren waited for an opening and then launched themselves into the crowd. At first, James' ankles buckled slightly, but he finally overcame that wobbly stance as he picked up a little speed. Still skaters were passing him, and Mr. Speed went back to his fast mode as long as the woman was not watching. James felt his presence as he came dangerously close on his fast trip around the rink. He paid close attention to nearby skaters and Lauren, not wanting to collide and look silly. What he did not need was a fall, associated broken bones and the subsequent ribbing he would get from the shift. A boy, probably seven or eight, cut across his path at a slow pace and James barely missed him. An elderly couple with arms locked passed him, giving him a good margin. He admired their fluid motion as they slid through narrow gaps between skaters.

James finally started to look around him and was mesmerised by Lauren's skating, so graceful and smooth, whilst he almost clunked along. Her long blonde hair flowed as she gained speed by her flawless action, leaning forward and swinging her arms gently. She wore a short, light blue jacket. Her legs were covered in leggings which showed off their length, along with how shapely and toned they were. James was yet again amazed at her striking appearance. Lauren could tell James was looking at her, so she turned near him and skated backward a short distance. She jumped and landed frontward to continue. Her lips were full and turned into a scowl, her blue eyes piercing.

A pre-teen girl cut in front of James and he had to veer right to avoid hitting her. He managed to avoid a collision, but the turn was too sudden for him and he went down. Sliding a few feet, he managed to avoid injury, but he was in Mr. Speed's wild path. The fast skater jumped over him, but his skate caught James's forehead, causing him to see stars. Mr. Speed never even bothered to stop and check on him.

James touched his forehead and was relieved there was no blood. With a rather sore head, James watched Lauren skate toward him and then make a sideways skidding stop, a shower of ice chips covering him. She went to one knee, her hair swaying forward, her brow creased with worry furrows.

"Oh, sorry about the ice shower," Lauren said, and then continued as she gingerly touched his forehead.

"There's no cut, but you'll have an egg if we don't get an ice pack on it. Let's get you over to the bench."

Lauren helped James up. He relished her gentle touch and marvellous strength as she hoisted him to his feet and led him to the bench. Once safely there, she laid her hand on his shoulder.

"Stay here. I'm going to get an ice pack."

James watched her skate away toward a steward to ask for a first aid box and ice pack.

"Hold that against your bump."

Lauren decided she would have a word with Mr Speed. He was going faster than ever, but she easily overtook him. James was amazed at her speed, and even more amazed when she grabbed his coat collar and did her sideways skid, bringing him to an abrupt stop. The man looked down at her as she spoke to him and was joined by a steward. He seemed to ignore her and the steward, but that did not last long. Lauren grabbed him more firmly and actually dragged him off, handling him like a rag doll. He wasted no time removing his skates and putting on his shoes while she stood with her hands on her slender waist, glaring down at him. That done, she returned to James and sat beside him.

"We may have to get that checked at A&E to make sure you don't have a concussion."

She removed the ice pack and peered at his bruise.

"Going down, still have a nice war wound," she laughed.

Lauren got up and went back on the ice. James watched her graceful skating for another few minutes and then removed his skates. Lauren did a few more laps before returning and asking James how he felt.

James said, "I am ok. Got a bit of headache."

James felt that his pride had been hurt more. He returned his skates, and the attendant made a comment about the rather large egg on his forehead. Lauren looked at James and felt sorry for him.

She centred her gaze on his lips, moved her hair to her ear, and he gently pulled her to meet his lips. She responded by resting on her hand on his cheek during the kiss. When they parted, numbness overtook James, as he feared he had stepped way over his bounds.

"Oh, Lauren, I'm sorry. I shouldn't have. . ." She touched his lips with her forefinger.

"Shhh!"

She initiated another kiss, this one stretching a bit longer. They stood face to face with hands clasped. Lauren then moved away and said,

"I think you are ok now. Fancy going and getting something to eat?"

James was confused yet again; was that a kiss of passion or a kiss to make him feel better?

James did not want to say anything after the kiss at the nightclub so, yet again, they both pretended nothing had happened.

Chapter Ten – With the "Sarg"

Lauren was off on an operation and Ian and Chris were working together. This meant James was with Sergeant Bloor tonight. Sergeant Andy Bloor had 20 years' service - ten years as a PC, then a further ten as a response sergeant. He could be quite sharp at times, but was the first to back up his shift and solve any issues. He could also be quite cynical, and when in a bad mood, was best avoided at all costs. Firm but fair and very professional probably summed the sergeant up well. His level of knowledge was outstanding; he really was a police oracle and pretty much had an answer to any police-related question you asked.

James felt a bit nervous about being out with the sergeant. He did not want to show himself up. The "Sarg" was quite chatty tonight, telling James what he had been up to and making the odd rude comment along the way. James actually enjoyed the banter and began to feel more comfortable being out with him. Although the sergeant did ask some knowing questions about how James and Lauren were getting on, almost as if he knew something was going on.

After an hour or so patrolling, the sergeant noticed two cars pulled up in a layby and his instinct was that something was not right.

"James, I really am not sure about these two cars. As soon as we pull up, can you do a PNC check."

James replied, "Yep, no problem."

On pulling up, James noticed there was a Volvo estate, and the sergeant said,

"That looks like one of our old traffic cars. I am sure I have seen the number plate before."

They both got out of the car and a male quickly walked up to them, saying,

"Hello officer, what is going on? I already have an officer with me, checking my details."

"Oh, right," said the sergeant.

Meanwhile, James had checked the details of the Volvo and saw that it was registered to a private owner, a Liam Fisher.

The sergeant went over to Liam and asked,

"What is going here?"

Liam replied, "Just stopped this chap for using his mobile phone. On an operation."

Sergeant Bloor said, "Oh, you are? What is your collar number and name?"

Liam replied, "I am 4127 Fisher. I work with roads policing," sounding very confident and sure of himself.

"Oh, OK, I know your sergeant very well - Steve Stanley. I will give him a quick ring."

James, like the sergeant, thought that nothing made any sense. The sergeant duly got on his mobile phone and spoke to Steve, who confirmed what he thought - Liam was not an actual police officer. He had just bought the ex-unmarked traffic police car. This was not the first time he had been caught either. Only 6 months ago, he had been sacked from the specials for putting blue lights on his own car, pretending to be a traffic officer and actually pulling cars over or driving at speed with his blue lights flashing.

Due to the type of case and the fact that it was of interest to roads policing, they came over and arrested Liam for impersonating a police officer. They were going to look at other offences he could be charged with as well.

With that, the sergeant and James went back on their travels, and it was not long before they got a call. It was a report of a woman called Janice, who had been missing and had now been found. She was outside some houses on a new estate and needed to be returned home.

She was reported as having mental health problems and this was not the first time she had been found on the same housing estate.

On arrival, James and Sergeant Bloor found her walking along a path outside some brand new houses that were not quite finished, and they went to speak to her. She was quite small but had a very full figure. She explained that she was looking at her new house and was due to move in with her husband next week. She said she was 16, when she actually looked about 40.

The minute James said that they needed to take her home, she became distressed.

"Please don't take me home. I don't want to go home, I want to go back to my mummy. I hate it there."

James did his best to calm her down whilst Sergeant Bloor got on the radio to arrange to take her back. James did very well, getting her calm and into the police car. On the way back, she chatted away and was very calm, until they got close to where she lived and she started to become quite distressed.

As soon as they pulled up, James opened the car door to get her out; she flatly refused and had to be helped out. The moment she got out of the car, she went flat on her back on the ground and started to thrash about violently. James and the sergeant tried to lift her, but her own strength and weight made it near impossible for the two of them to do so.

The thrashing had caused her top and bra to come off, and James did his best to protect her modesty whilst some nurses from the hospice came out to help. With this commotion going on outside, something came flying through the glass of a downstairs window, followed by shouting.

James asked one of the nurses, "What is going on?"

He replied, "Barbra hates the police and thinks you are coming to take her away. She will be alright once she has a tablet or two."

James could see another nurse trying to shove a pill and some water down Barbra's throat. Barbra was painfully thin and had curly grey hair; she looked to be in her late 50s. Her eyes were wild, and her shouting was closer to a scream than anything else.

By now, Janice had calmed down. With two nurses, the sergeant and James were able to get her up and walk her inside. They sat her in a chair, and within a matter of minutes, she was fast asleep.

With that job done, James and Sergeant Bloor headed back to their area across the city to have some much-deserved food.

On the way back, Sergeant Bloor decided to tell James what it was like being a police officer 20 years ago. He started with a story about when he was young in service and working nights. He was on foot patrol outside a public house when two men came rolling out of the front door, scrapping for all they were worth. Now, any experienced officer would have let them get on with it for a bit before breaking them up and picking up the pieces, but the sergeant thought he could sort it out.

Walking over, he split up the two males, only to have one of them, a particularly strong and wiry young man, turn on him. This started a lengthy wrestling match between the sergeant and this young man, which resulted in the whole pub turning out as excited and rowdy spectators and the sergeant being half pushed and half thrown through a plate-glass shop window.

As he went through the window, he involuntarily curled up his toes because a large shard of glass fell onto the toe of his boot, cutting it off and leaving him with his toes hanging out. Other than a small cut on his lip, the sergeant said he was uninjured. What started off as a relatively minor incident had ended up, thanks to his intervention, as quite a considerable disturbance. The man with whom the sergeant had been fighting was subsequently fined. The sergeant learnt a valuable lesson - never rush into a situation and, if necessary, get help prior to intervening.

Then he went on to tell a funny story about a fellow colleague who was now an inspector, but had been a PC at the time. He was driving a Ford Escort panda car and was responding to a call. As he accelerated on a long straight road, the car left the carriageway and ended up perched on a stone wall. There were no other vehicles involved, thankfully. The funny part was, when asked to explain the accident to his sergeant, he replied, "I turned on the blue light, and the car went round." In those days, panda cars had a single rotating flashing blue light on the roof.

James laughed, but understood the points the sergeant was getting across; he was trying to make sure James did not fall into the same pitfalls he had, especially with the increased accountability in the modern police service and being more susceptible to litigation.

CHAPTER ELEVEN – WORRY

Lauren was meeting up today with an old friend who had just got back from holiday. Lauren had not seen her in ages, even though they were close and had known each other for years. As Lauren's career had taken off, Tracy had seen less and less of her as they were both cops and worked different shifts. Lauren was looking forward to catching up, although unsure if she should mention James or not.

"Tracy, this is absolutely beautiful," Lauren said, caressing the large agate stone with her fingertip. The vintage sterling silver bangle surrounded her wrist with elegance and class. "You're too good to me."

"I'm glad you like it. There were so many to choose from; they make them right there on the island."

Lauren stood and leaned over the cafe table to give her best friend a hug. "I more than like it. I love it." She returned to her seat.

"You have to plan to accompany me next year, Lauren. You are a workaholic. So far, you have missed Jamaica, Costa Rica, and now Mexico. You are in the prime of your life. Enjoy it while you can."

"I know, I know. You are right on all points, but I want to hear about your trip. Were there any good-looking guys in Baja?"

Tracy picked up a napkin and fanned herself. "My eyeballs are sore from ogling." Lauren laughed.

Lauren admired her friend's crazy sense of humour, but her heavy-laden heart would not allow her the luxury of laughing.

"Next month, I'm going to have a party. I want to meet this mystery friend of yours," Tracy said, eyeing her intently. "He sounds interesting."

"I... I wouldn't exactly call him a mystery. We both have busy schedules."

Tracy took her wallet from her purse. "Well, mark your calendar. No excuses. I want to meet him."

"Put that away, I'll take care of the tab." Thankful for the distraction, Lauren placed some money on the table.

Tracy leaned forward, her hazel eyes full of mischief. "I'm not letting you off the hook. Are you going to bring your mysterious man to the party?"

"Maybe, but don't expect me to wear a bathing suit. I have to lose a few pounds."

"Lauren, please. Men are all over you everywhere we go. Your beautiful face and body are to die for. Besides, wearing a size fourteen is average these days."

"Humph, if you say so. Why are you a size ten if twelve is so popular?"

Tracy laughed. "Talk to God about that. I wish I had a bigger rear to strut. Seriously, I think you are gorgeous. I also think you need to take more time out to enjoy yourself."

If she only knew how much fun Lauren had had lately. "I'll keep it in mind," Lauren said, trying to hide what she was dying to tell Tracy.

"Good. I'd better get going; I'm picking Lois up early from the sitter. I promised to take her for ice cream. Would you like to join us? She hasn't seen her godmother in almost two weeks."

"No, I can't. I have to finish some paperwork at work. Would it be okay if I picked her up on Saturday for a couple of hours?"

Tracy stood, smoothing her black dress. "Of course, that'll give me time to run a few errands."

Lauren's insides flip-flopped. She could not let this go any further. "Um, Tracy, can we talk a few minutes before you leave?"

Tracy slid back into her chair. "Sure. What's up?"

A hush fell over the small cafe, as if anticipating her words. Lauren played with the edges of a napkin before lifting her gaze to Tracy. She took a trembling breath. "The mystery guy I'm seeing isn't someone I just met. I have known him for quite a while. We work together; we started a while ago."

Tracy gave a startled look. "James? As in your student officer?"

Lauren said, "Yes, it has been really hard to keep it quiet at work"

Tracy was concerned as she knew it was only six months since Lauren had split up with Dean and, being a police officer herself at a different station, she knew that romances could cause many issues.

Lauren tightened the belt on her robe as she sprinted across the room to answer the door. Please let it be James. She had tried calling him earlier but he had not answered. Breathless from emotions and the short run, she pulled the door open. Her heart split down the middle. James stood on the other side. His good looks held her captivated, and all he would become in her life enveloped her. She wanted to throw herself into his strong arms, while also wishing he would disappear.

He smiled. "Are you going to invite me in?"

"Yes." As soon as the door closed, he drew her into his arms. "I thought you were popping round?"

"Something came up." She gently pushed away from the comfort of his arms and walked into the living room.

"I hope nothing serious."

"Serious enough."

"Do you want to talk about it?"

"James, listen. This isn't going to work. I think we need to cool it for a while."

He frowned. "What do you mean, cool it?"

"I mean we shouldn't see each other right now. I need to sort a few things in my mind." She turned her back to him. Her mouth and heart were going in different directions. No man had ever made her feel as special as he did. She had fallen hard and James was rapidly becoming her rock - something Lauren grew scared of. She was also worried about the effect of her a career, as being a police officer was all she had ever wanted to do.

James circled and stood in front her. He took her hands in his. "A few hours ago, you were fine. What is this really about?"

"It's just best for all concerned."

He released her hands. "For all concerned? I can't imagine being without you. And this is all you have to say?"

She pressed her fingers against her swollen eyes. "Tracy knows."

"Is this the reason you don't want to see me?"

"Yes, for the most part."

"Lauren, you're the woman I want to be with. I want us to move in together." His lips tilted in a smile. "I want you to cook my tea."

Lauren gave a wry smile, but it did not stop what she was feeling inside.

Butterflies swarmed her stomach. The thought of moving in with James left her dizzy and elated, but the ugly reality would not allow it to sink in. "It won't work. Think about the effect this will have on our careers."

James' brows drew together. "We're not doing anything wrong. You are entitled to find happiness and again, I have found that happiness with you. Surely she can't hold that against us." He reached out and held Lauren's shoulders. "Please, don't give up what we have."

Lauren pursed her lips. "I'm sorry, but we can't be more than friends. It's best that you leave."

James' hands dropped to his sides, emotions stirring in the depths of his eyes. He turned and walked out. Lauren held the wall as a wave of emotion hit her.

For the second time, Lauren had cold feet and was more worried about her career than her love life. James felt like he was on a roller-coaster ride.

Chapter Twelve – Error of Judgment

It was a Friday night and James had been on since 3pm, he had attended a few minor incidents on his own and was enjoying the freedom of being single crewed.

At 7pm, his sergeant asked him if he did not mind taking a special constable out, as there was no one else free. James did feel a bit apprehensive, as he was still quite new in service himself without taking a month old special out.

James went back to the station to pick Jessica the special up. She seemed quite shy and quiet and reminded James of how he felt when he first started. Sitting huddle in the corner of the parade room, she looked like a startled rabbit as James approached her.

"Hiya Jessica, I am James looks like you have drawn the short straw and been paired with me."

Jessica just gave a shy smile.

"Are you ready to go out then?" asked James.

Jessica replied, "Yes"

James had wondered why he had not ever thought about being a special first. They pretty much did exactly what he did and was, a great way to learn about the job. They could choose the hours they wanted to work as well. The only downside was that they did not get paid, other than a couple of, "uniform carriers" he had been amazed at how professional and how well they did their job. A couple were nearly as good as any regular officer, although specials had neither the training or the time to be able to do everything a full-time cop could do.

Jessica and James left to go out on patrol, Jessica wanted to be a regular officer when they started to recruit again and was keen to learn and do well. Out on patrol they soon got called to reports of anti-social behaviour. Jessica seemed keen to learn and watched James intently has he did stop checks and spoke to the group of teenagers about their behaviour.

At 9pm, they went in for snap and Jessica wanted to give her boyfriend a call. He was not quite so keen on her being a cop. It felt strange to James being the teacher and not the student. After snap, which was police speak for something to eat, they went back out on patrol.

James and Jessica chatted away, and it turned out James's dad had taught her a few years back. As they pulled up at a set of traffic light next to the Archers Arms, James noticed a large group jostling with each other and then a male in a grey jumper seemed to hit another male.

As soon as the lights changed, James drove the car round to the front of the pub and got out with Jessica following a short distance behind. James went straight to the male and tried to arrest him for assault. In doing so, his mates surrounded James. Then his girlfriend tried to pull the male away, and before he knew it the males mates had were saying.

"He ain't done anything, let him go."

The male replied, "I've not done anything, wrong, we're just messing around."

James could tell he was in a dodgy situation and wondered why he had rushed in, and then suddenly the girlfriend of the man James was trying to arrest was trying to pull him away. In doing so - they all ended up in a pile of the floor. Realising he was in over his head and in need of assistance; he pushed his emergency button and screamed.

"Got a fight at the Archers Arms need assistance"

Everything then went into slow motion.

By now, Jessica had screamed at the crowd, "WILL YOU BACKOFF NOW" as James managed to get to his feet. Still surrounded James drew his BATON shouting, "BACKOFF BACKOFF". In what seemed like an age to arrive backup finally appeared first two, then four and followed by armed response.

Another officer got kicked by a female as a bigger crowd grew and the melee ensued.

James pointed out the instigator of the affray, and he was promptly arrested. James helped armed response handcuff another male who was resisting arrest, and it took three of them just to get the handcuffs on.

A van arrived to take the most violent offenders away, and within 15 minutes, it was all over. James had ended up with a more compliant prisoner in the back of his car.

Once James and Jessica had the prisoner booked in, they went back to the Archers Arms to seize CCTV of the fight. Back at the station James was ribbed by Ian and James for starting a fight, which James thought was not too far from the truth. Maybe he should have spoken to the male first before trying to arrest him?

In total 25 cops had attended the fight some from other areas, as an assistance call from a cop is serious and everyone drops what they are doing and rushes to help.

James knew he was going to be off late so made a start on his witness statement along with a few other cops. Thankfully, Chris had offered to take the lead and said he would compile and complete all the paperwork.

It took James well over an hour and half to get his statement written and help Jessica write her statement. James passed his statement on to Chris to read and check.

I am a Police Constable 3468 SOWMAN of Hampshire Police currently stationed at Otherton Police station. At 22:55 hours on Friday 6th March 2011, I was conducting uniformed patrol duties in company with SC 5291 ANDERSON in the Otherton area. At this time, I was driving a fully liveried Police vehicle along KNIGHT ROAD, OTHERTON and was waiting to turn right onto HILL ROAD at the traffic lights.

The ARCHERS ARMS PUB public house known locally as AA was located on my right-hand side. The property fronts onto HILL ROAD, one side is adjacent to KNIGHT ROAD and the rear of these public house backs onto OTHERTON ROAD. To my right, I noticed a large group of males, approximately 10 – 12 males that were on the pavement between the side of the ARCHERS ARM and the safety railings.

There looked to be two separate groups, and I could see about four people jostling each other. The four were behaving aggressively towards each other, and they looked like they were being abusive, their faces were contorted and confrontational to each other. I observed this group whilst waiting at the traffic lights for about two minutes and became concerned that a fight was breaking out, as the group continued to jostle each other, and I feared things were going to escalate. I passed on what I had seen to Command and Control via my radio.

I would estimate the group was 20 feet away from me, and I had a clear unobstructed view of the group. The weather was clear, and the street lighting illuminated the streets to a good degree. I saw a male in a grey top throw a punch at a male in a white top. From now on, I will refer to the male in the grey top as male 1. The male in the white top I now know to be Tom HIGGINS DOB 16/09/1973. I would describe HIGGINS as a white male with a shaved head and approximately 6 feet tall. HIGGINS was of a medium build and spoke with a local accent, aged in his early thirties. HIGGINS was wearing a knitted white polo neck jumper and plain dark-blue jeans.

Male 1 I would describe as white and of a medium build, he was between 5'08" and 5'10" tall. Aged in his early thirties, he had short cropped dark hair, and he was wearing a short-sleeved grey t-shirt with white piping around the neck area. I have not seen this male before, nor do I know him, but I would recognise him again.

HIGGINS then shoved male 1 away, causing him to stumble backwards. Male 1 then came forward again and tried to throw another punch at HIGGINS. HIGGINS then lunged forward towards male 1 and at this point the traffic lights changed, and I moved off to park the Police vehicle on HILL ROAD. I lost visual contact with the group for about one minute whilst parking the vehicle in a safe place.

I then got out of the Police vehicle by the railings on HILL ROAD opposite the entrance to the public house. I saw the same group of people standing on the pavement by KNIGHT ROAD. However, I could only see three people at this stage. I could see HIGGINS; he was about 30 feet away from where I was standing with no obstructions. I saw HIGGINS use both his arms to push another male, hard. HIGGINS appeared to push the male deliberately with significant force.

At 23:00 hours, I ran over to HIGGINS and said, "I am arresting you for affray" CAUTION to which he said, "I'VE NOT DONE ANYTHING, WE'RE JUST MESSING AROUND!" I put my right hand on HIGGINS's left shoulder and my left hand on HIGGINS's right wrist in a prisoner escort technique to lead HIGGINS away from the scene to diffuse the situation.

HIGGINS immediately resisted my attempt to lead him away from the scene by standing still and tensing his body. HIGGINS was heavily into drink, I could smell intoxicating liqueur on his breath, and his eyes were watery. HIGGINS was very aggressive in both his manner and tone. HIGGINS had an aggressive look in his eyes as if he had just been involved in a fight or intense argument with another person.

At this point, I became surrounded by a number of males who began to shout at me "HE HASN'T DONE ANYTHING!" At least, two males got within fifteen centimetres of my face and repeatedly shouted "HE HASN'T DONE ANYTHING!" I immediately began to be concerned for the safety of SC ANDERSON and myself at this point. The males had closed down my reactionary gap and were becoming increasingly hostile. I still had HIGGINS in an escort hold.

At this point, a white female approached, who I now know to be Christine JONES DOB 03/02/1972 who I would describe as having shoulder length or longer blonde hair, of slim build aged in her thirties, around 5'04" – 5'06" tall. JONES was wearing a white t-shirt type top, black skirt, and black tights with black heeled boots and came to the left side of me and threw her arms around HIGGINS's waist in order to prevent me from taking HIGGINS away.

JONES, who appeared quite emotional continued to violently pull at HIGGINS's waist causing him to fall backwards, onto the pavement. JONES also fell onto her back, and HIGGINS fell onto JONES. I kept hold of HIGGINS to try and prevent him from falling over with JONES. This pulled me off balance and dragged me down to the point where I was down on one knee. I immediately let go of HIGGINS as I was now very concerned and felt both PC 8088 ANDERSON and I were in grave danger. I immediately pressed my emergency button on the airwave radio to summon assistance.

I managed to get back to my feet, and I saw SC ANDERSON shout loudly at the crowd. "WILL YOU GET BACK!" The crowd then moved around towards the front door of the ARCHERS ARMS pub, JONES was still holding onto HIGGINS and they were resting up against the side of the ARCHERS ARMS pub.

I would estimate there were now about 12 – 14 people out on the pavement in front of the ARCHERS ARMS pub. PC 2998 COLLINS arrived, and he was standing less than two feet in front of JONES and HIGGINS. He attempted to split up JONES and HIGGINS, JONES reacted and kicked PC 2998 COLLINS in a toe poke frontward kick to PC 2998 COLLINS's right knee to make him back off.

PC COLLINS backed away, to prevent further assault. As he did this the crowd began to shout angrily and aggressively "DON'T TOUCH HER SHE IS A WOMAN!" Both PC 2998 COLLINS and I were totally surrounded by the crowd who were increasingly hostile towards

Police. I became fearful for my safety so I withdrew my Police issue baton and placed the baton over my right shoulder and shouted at the crowd "BACK OFF! BACK OFF! BACK OFF! BACK OFF!" I felt the situation was escalating and getting out of control.

Other officers arrived very quickly and began to disperse the crowd. I located HIGGINS shortly after the initial crowd had been dispersed and reminded HIGGINS he was under COLLINS for affray. I handcuffed HIGGINS to the rear and double locked the handcuffs and checked for tightness. C division officers then conveyed HIGGINS to the CUSTODY suite in a marked Police van.

At this time, there was still a large crowd with parts of the crowd still hostile. I was advised that there was already a prisoner in our Police vehicle. Then in company with PC ANDERSON I conveyed a male I now know to be Antony WOOD into CUSTODY where the custody Sergeant authorized his detention.

Later I returned to the ARCHERS ARMS with SC 5291 ANDERSON, who seized CCTV footage from the premises.

Chris was quite impressed with James's statement and was pretty much spot on. With that, everything James needed to do completed, James helped Chris finish off the rest of paperwork, including the crime report and handover file needed by the morning shift who would interview the suspects. They managed to get off at 3am. On the way out Chris said.

"Typical 10 minutes of action followed by four hours of paperwork"

James nodded in agreement - one of the first things he had been amazed at was the amount of paperwork a police officer undertakes.

Chapter Thirteen – New Horizons

Lauren gave her large shoulder bag, one last shove and said a silent prayer of thanks as she let it slide into her crammed car boot. All she wanted was to get away and move into her new house.

She dropped down in her car seat, ran a hand through her hair and sighed. At the same time, a wave of relief washed over her. All she wanted was to be alone.

Lauren hated what she'd become since the pending divorce. It was one of the main reasons why she had decided to pack up and move away, even if it was not that far away. She needed a fresh start, a chance to reinvent herself in a place where the memory of her ex-husband Dean's infidelities would not shadow her every step of the way. A rural setting was exactly what she needed-a place where no one knew her business, furthermore no one cared.

Her pulse thudded in her ears as the gravity of the situation finally hit her. She was starting over, moving away where the only person she knew locally was an old school friend, and she had got back in touch a year ago. Since she had made the decision to move out two months ago, she had tried not to think about what would come next. Sure, she had a good sum of money coming from the divorce settlement, but then what? She had her job, which she loved, and some good friends in and out of work, especially Tracy.

For four years, she had been so busy being a wife, obsessing over when, and if to have a baby. She had not had a chance to figure out who she was or what she wanted from life. However, now she had all the time in the world and it scared her to death.

Lauren's chest tightened uncomfortably, and her breaths came quick and shallow. Whom was she kidding? She was not the type of person who could start over. It was hard to face the uncertainty of the future and the possibility of failing at what she did next just as she had failed at her marriage.

She started her car and drove off to her new house and new life.

After she had unpacked Lauren needed to go and get some groceries from the Tesco Express around the corner, still stunned by what she had just done and feeling a little tender, she was in her own world.

A sudden bump on the elbow jolted Lauren back to reality. She glanced up at the source, a pair of brawny shoulders.

"I'm so sorry," the owner of the bag and the shoulders said as he craned his head to face her.

"That's okay," she mumbled, turning back to the shelf full of various types of bread.

However, he did not move on.

"Lauren? Lauren Reilly? Is that you?" Lauren heard him say.

She could not remember the last time anyone called her by her maiden name, so it took a minute to register that yes that was her name-again.

By the time Lauren looked up, the man had turned full circle and was making his way back up the aisle until he was beside her. Now able to get a good look at his face, a wave a familiarity washed over her.

"Laurence?" Lauren asked, feeling some of the tightness in her chest subsiding. "Oh my, Laurence Chapman. I have not seen you since… well school.

Laurence replied, "Has it been that long?"

Lauren and Laurence had gone to the same school along with the other friend Janice who lived in the village as well. Although they had not been close, with several mutual friends, they often found themselves hanging out in the same places, going to the same parties. Laurence looked much the same as he did when she last saw him. His light-brown hair was cut shorter now. He had managed to maintain the trim muscular physique that Lauren had secretly admired as a teen.

"It has. It has. How've you been?" he asked casually.

As she looked up into his brown eyes, Lauren thought about his question. How was she? She was alone for the first time in seven years. She was scared out of her mind. However, the realization suddenly hit her; she could handle this. After what she had been, through-she could handle anything.

"I'm okay, Laurence," she answered truthfully and explained she had just moved in after a recent break up. "And you?"

"I'm good thanks. I was just picking up some groceries on my way home from work."

Lauren chuckled, feeling more at ease than she had in some time.

He looked at her intently, his eyes searching her baby blues. "You know. It is weird; I was thinking about you the other day. It's really great to see you."

"Would you like to catch up sometime?" She was so shocked to hear the words come out of her mouth.

His lips spread into a smile. "Sure."

"Tell you what Lauren; I only live just round the corner why not pop round later? No point being alone on your first evening."

"Yes, that will be really nice," said Lauren, trying to hide that fact she really did not want to be at home alone on her first night.

Lauren went round to Laurence's, and she sat down on the black leather sofa. He had done well for himself. Set up his own security business and supplied door staff to all the clubs in the city. Laurence settled in beside her, and as they chatted about mutual friends and his life, Lauren felt warm, comfortable, and wondered why she had never considered dating Laurence in high school.

"So how come you are moving here? Last I heard you were married?"

The question hit her like a blow to the chest. It was a perfectly reasonable question. She knew. Most people their age were married. However, back where she had lived, everyone knew about the divorce, so she had not had to deal with the questions. She realised that now she was going to have to get used to it.

She took a deep breath. "No, I'm getting divorced, so it's just me."

Laurence's eyes filled with concern. "I'm sorry."

"Don't worry about it," she replied with a shrug of the shoulders. "Actually, I have moved here to start afresh, and to tell you the truth, I'm pretty nervous about the whole thing." It was the first time she had admitted it to anyone, and it made her feel a little better.

"Well, don't be." He replied. "It's a great area. You're going to love it."

Lauren felt really at ease in the first time for ages, and whilst she enjoyed Laurence's company, she could not help but think of James.

Laurence and Lauren chatted away into the early hours Lauren felt as if she had regained her past and her husband's affair that lead to the breakdown of the marriage was all in the past. This was six months ago a week before their big night out. She had kept everything hush even James did not know about her previous life and marriage and another reason she had backed off from James.

It was all too soon and then she had decided to give it a go but got cold feet and backed off. In doing so she had hurt James, now they hardly spoke and James would always work with Ian or Chris now he no longer needed to work directly with Lauren.

They would speak when they needed to on a professional level but the banter and friendship they had seemed to of drained away.

CHAPTER FOURTEEN – SHOT DEAD

James was paired up with Ian for this shift. Both James and Ian had become good friends. Ian was excellent at handling people, very rarely ever raising his voice or getting angry. The downside to being so big was that all the drunks wanted to take him on, and have a go whenever they went to drink related jobs.

Ian had been in the job nine years and was originally a PCSO before applying to be a full-time officer. He had made quite a few mistakes in his early years as a cop. Some of which had still not been forgotten. James found him to be very competent and very helpful. He was always happy and willing to take a special out or help them with some paperwork and had almost become James's second tutor after Lauren.

They had already attended an RTC were a large arctic lorry had turned on its side whilst going round a roundabout. It seemed the lorry had clipped a curb, and that had been enough to cause the trailer to flip onto its side taking the tractor unit with it. Luckily, it had flipped onto the side not the centre of the roundabout and no other vehicles were involved.

It was quite amazing to see such a large vehicle on its side and cover nearly half the roundabout. Ian actually said this was not uncommon, although the roundabout it usually happened on was due to the camber and too much speed leading to several arctic lorries over the years toppling over. This was the first time he had seen a lorry flip over on this roundabout.

The lorry driver was uninjured, although his pride was hurt a little; amazingly, the load of fridges the lorry was carrying seemed ok.

However, both James and some of the Fire Brigade were making rather bad fridge type jokes like, "There will have to be a price freeze now and it's a chilling sight in the back of that lorry."

The road would have to be closed to recover the lorry, Ian and James felt that would be best left to the early hours when traffic flow was minimal.

The RTC meant an accident card needed to be completed, and James offered to do this, as he wanted more practice. They were not that hard to do just a series of tick boxes and spaces for longer answers. Slightly more complex to fill out if it had been an injury accident.

However, that would have to wait though as they got the next call of a shooting. Armed response had already been dispatched, and Ian and James were told to stand off once in the area. So that armed response could check the scene and make sure it was safe for everyone else.

When armed responses arrived, there was no sign of the offenders. The person who phoned in the shooting had reported a silver car moving off at speed.

When James and Ian finally arrived at the scene, armed response had done their job and made sure no offenders were still on the scene before allowing any other officers and paramedics forward. It was then James and Ian's job to secure the area and set up a cordon.

A man in his thirties lay on his back in a large pool of blood in the hallway of a house, after being shot several times. His chest wounds were very obvious thorough his heavily blood stained shirt. He lived in a semi-detached house in one of the better areas of Otherton. The garden was slightly overgrown, but the rest of the house was neat and tidy. Nothing had been stolen from the house and there were no signs of forced entry either.

It was almost as if the man had opened the doors to his killers, and then been shot several times before his killers had made a quick getaway.

The man's estranged wife turned up and was quite hysterical and Ian calmed her down. He asked her if sure knew any reason why her husband would have been shot. All she knew was that he was in desperate need of £20,000 something to do with his business and had pleaded with her for the money. He had not long left her house when one of her husband's neighbours had rung to say what had happened.

James and Ian would now be on-scene preservation until CID arrived to take over, as this was a murder investigation. An officer would still be needed to guard the house whilst CID did their work though. Luckily, it was near the end of their shift so the night shift would have to send someone out to relive Ian and James.

There had been a recent rise in shootings in the area linked to drugs cartel that was putting fear of violence on a local council estate to take control of the drugs trade. This shooting could well be connected to another shooting.

When James and Ian were finally relieved, they chatted in the car about the shooting and how rumours of corrupt police officers, who were feeding intelligence to the cartel. Ian really hated corrupt officers as the media made a big song and dance of it and did not help the public's perception of the police either. Thankfully, they were rare and the service was quick to weed them out and ended up being thrown out the service.

A lot of what was going on had been kept secret from the rank and file officers other than general information. Rumour was that Mi5 was involved as well as the national crime squad.

James thought he might like to be a detective or DC in a few years, but for now he did enjoy response, it was very varied and you never knew what was going to happen from one shift to the next.

James was doing well, his Sergeant had done his first performance review, and overall praised James for how he had got stuck in and had picked up things well. To James's surprise, even saying he would make an excellent cop and glad he was part of the shift.

James had felt down since the breakup with Lauren. It was a nice uplift; James did wonder if the shift knew what had happened between himself and Lauren? If so, then they were certainly not letting on.

Chapter Fifteen – Making Up

Lauren stroked her eyelids with eye shadow. The shimmering colour brought out the softness of her blue eyes. Satisfied with the perfect application of her makeup, she turned sideways in the mirror to inspect the fitted grey dress that rested just above her knees. She had splurged at Warehouse and it was well worth it. After slipping her feet into a pair of strappy black platform heels, she walked through her door.

The cool evening breeze greeted her as she strolled to her car. She had decided that she was going to go and see James and try to sort things out. She had missed their chats and even at work rarely saw James since he had started going out on his own, and working nights with Ian.

Lauren stood in the doorway of James's house, as he opened the door; he was a sight to behold. His broad shoulders filled his shirt. She could not stand being apart from him another moment.

James stared at Lauren shock registering on his face. His gaze left a sizzling trail as it moved over her curves and down to her feet. He lent against the doorframe, "What can I do for you, Lauren?"

"Can I come in" asked Lauren.

"I suppose so," said James.

Inside James felt quite pleased that she had come to see him, but did not want to show it. He still felt angry at the way she had treated him.

Lauren's heels clicked against the wooden floors in the hall as she followed James into his living room. The hardness in his eyes took her aback.

She swallowed the lump in her throat. "James, I'm sorry."

"I'm not sure what you want me to say."

"I just want you to hear me out."

He folded his hands on his desk. "Okay, oaky go for it."

"I thought that disappearing and not seeing you would change the way I feel about you. Instead, it proved how much I need you in my life. I know I hurt you by throwing our love aside, and if you give me a chance, I promise I'll never let anyone or anything comes between us again."

James stood and shoved his chair back.

"For a month I've been to hell and back, unable to sleep, eat or think, made worse by having to see you at work and be professional. You just waltz in here unexpectedly and ask me to give you another chance. Well, I am not a light switch that you can turn on and off when you are ready. You hurt me. I thought a couple of weeks ago we could get through this, but I was wrong."

Lauren touched his arm. "I know how much I hurt you and I want to try to make it up to you."

In one swift move, James drew her close to his thumping heart. He wove his fingers through her hair. "I don't think I can survive losing you a second time."

Melting in his arms, Lauren held him tight. The warmth of his breath against her ear sent shivers down her spine.

"Don't ever put me through that again," he commanded in a hoarse voice.

She held his face in her hands and lifted her lips toward his, "Never."

Then James replied "Where are you taking me too, then? I hope it's not McDonalds dressed like that? Mind you a McDonald's drive thru can be expensive if you have to buy a car first!"

Lauren burst into laughter and realised why she had fallen for James in the first place. It would take James sometime to feel settled with Lauren, as at the back of his mind was the nagging doubt that she might have another funny turn and leave him heartbroken.

Chapter Sixteen – Driver Training

The shift, as well as the whole police station, now knew James and Lauren were together. They had suffered all the banter, and James was glad to be away on his three-week driver-training course. The course would allow him to use blue lights and drive at speed to respond to emergencies. It meant three weeks of nine to five, the downside being that he could not see Lauren easily when she was on afternoons and nights and his training was during the day.

The first day, they all had a safety briefing and were given a theory test before going out in pairs with an advanced driving instructor to assess their ability. James did feel like he was on his driving test, and at the end, the instructor gave him a debrief.

Overall, James' driving was not too bad, but he was told that his steering needed some work and he was a bit sharp on the brakes. The first week was spent learning advanced driving techniques. James was surprised at how many bad habits he had picked up over the years.

The other part James found difficult at first was commenting on his driving. He had to say exactly what he was doing and what he had seen as he was driving. It took the best part of the first week to get used to it and for the instructor to be happy.

Saturday and Sunday were spent revising and going through what he had learnt, although he did manage to see Lauren and his family. James had yet to introduce Lauren to his family.

Monday morning came round in a flash, and this week they would start to drive at speed. The instructors really pushed hard and told James off for driving too slowly or for not making overtakes when it was safe to do so. It was all about making progression in a safe and smooth manner. The first couple of times, James was terrified at driving so fast.

James had not always been a cautious driver and had driven pretty fast and pretty dangerously when he was younger, but a bad accident had changed all that when he wrote off his first car, a SEAT Ibiza, after he rolled it in an accident. It gave James the shock, he needed to calm down and drive more slowly.

Now, James was being told to drive fast again, although in a much more controlled way, and he was being taught all the road sense he should have had when he first learnt to drive.

At the end of the three weeks, James passed the course and got his ticket to be a grade one driver. James felt elated, even though it had been a very tough three weeks and he had come close to failing.

Lauren was working all weekend so they had little time to catch up, but James was shattered after an intensive two weeks of training. Other than visiting his parents, James spent most of the weekend watching DVDs and playing on his Xbox.

However, on the Saturday, James decided it was time to go out and buy a new car. He would have gone for a Ford Focus but he drove them every day at work and fancied something a little more special.

He did the rounds of Ford, Vauxhall, Fiat, even Audi. The car that caught his eye was a BMW 1 series; a new one was way out of his price range, but a nearly new 09 plate 118d M Sport had caught his eye. It was a three door in white, a bit out of his price range but well worth it. James knew he would have to do some overtime to pay for it though. He negotiated what he thought was a decent deal and got his monthly payments to roughly what he wanted. He would be able to pick it up the following week.

It was strange to be back with the shift after three weeks away, but it was also nice to be back. Everyone congratulated James on passing the course, and James was a bit apprehensive about his first time driving at speed with the blue lights, responding to an emergency.

Chris had brought some cakes to have at briefing to celebrate; Ian, being his usual joker self, had brought James some L-plates. The comments had died down about Lauren and James and had moved onto PC Adams, who had crashing a car into a gate.

Sergeant Bloor also told James that they had the gunman who shot Kevin Doughty a month ago. It was all to do with an unpaid £20,000 loan from a loan shark that had originally been £5000, and the debt had been brought up by the cartel. Unable to pay, Kevin was made an example of and shot six times in the chest. The cost of life to the cartel was "very cheap," James thought.

Out on his own, James had been sent to interview a man charged with assault the previous night and had been given the proverbial handover. However, when he got there, he was told that the solicitor had been delayed and would not be there for another two hours at least.

There was no point in James hanging around, so he went back out on patrol and it was not long before he got his first immediate call. A child had been knocked down by a car near to a school. James gingerly pressed the 999 button to get his blue lights and pressed on his horn for the whaler. He soon found his feet. He did not want to go too fast, but could make good progress. The job he was going to filled him with dread. There was nothing worse than going to any accident involving a child.

On arrival, the ambulance was already there. A small group of people was standing on the side of the road. James got out and went to find out what had happened. Ian was already on his way, along with Lauren, and had asked for an update as soon as possible.

The driver made himself known and James asked him to sit in his car. It seems the mother of the girl had pulled up to let her out of the car, then she had just run out into the road without looking. The driver thankfully was driving slowly, due to it being a 20mph school zone. The girls seemed to be OK other than some cuts and bruises. The car had a big dent in the bonnet and seemed to have come off worse.

Ian and Lauren turned up and Ian offered to breathalyse the driver. The breath test proved negative. Lauren controlled the flow of traffic, with one side of the road being blocked.

James went into the back of the ambulance to get the girl's details and see what her injuries were. She had been very lucky, only suffering cuts and grazes to her arms and legs. She looked very shocked and was complaining of feeling sick, but otherwise she was OK.

James went back out and reported everything back to control so they could update the incident log. Then it was just a case of waiting for the ambulance to go before James could resume.

James had just enough time to get the accident card done before heading off back to custody to interview the male charged with assault.

This was James's fourth interview, although he had sat in on quite a few with Lauren. He wrote up his plan using TED, Tell me, Explain, Describe questions along the 5 WH, what, when, why, who, how.

James met and had a chat with the solicitor to explain the evidence and offence in the initial disclosure before taking the offender, David Adams, into the interview room.

James loaded two cassettes into the tape recorder and pressed play.

"I am PC 3468 Sowman. The date is April 9th. The time is 09:45

This interview is being recorded at Allenton Police Station and may be given in evidence if the case comes to trial.

I am interviewing David Adams.

Please state your full name, date of birth and address."

"I am David Adams, born 23rd June 1990."

"If a solicitor is present, state your name and the firm you represent."

"Carole Ford from Bartia Best."

"There are no other persons present in this interview.

You do not have to say anything. But it may harm your defence if you do not mention when questioned something you later rely on in court. Anything you do say may be given in evidence.

Do you understand?"

"Yes, I understand."

"The reason for this interview is because you have been arrested on suspicion of assault at the Nelsons arms, Otherton, on 8th April 2011.

I wish to speak to you about the comments made at the time of your arrest, prior to your arrival at custody."

You said, "It was not my fault, I was just defending myself." Do you agree this was said?"

"I cannot remember saying that."

"This is my opportunity to question you with regards to this matter. It is also your opportunity to give an explanation if you wish.

I am investigating an offence of assault.

I want your account for what happened."

"I was out drinking with my friends when this bloke came by and started being abusive. I asked him to leave us alone but he would not go. We finished our drinks and decided to go somewhere else. The man followed me out of the door and was in my face, shouting at me. I then pushed him away, to which he tried to hit me in my face. I managed to move and hit him back, and the next minute he was on the floor."

"Why did you not just walk away or call the police?"

"I tried to walk away, but as I said, he got into my face and I tried to push him away. I acted in self-defence."

"I must inform you that a court may draw a proper inference if you fail or refuse to answer satisfactorily any questions.

A record is being made of the interview, and it may be given in evidence if you are brought to trial.

I have explained to you what may occur. Do you understand what I have said?"

"Yes."

"It means that if you are reported or charged for the offence, and you have failed to answer these questions, the magistrate or jury can ask themselves the question, why didn't they explain when given the chance? Whatever they consider the answer to be, it can be taken into account when deciding guilt or innocence.

Do you wish to clarify anything?"

"No, other than it was self-defence."

"Have you said all you wish to say about this matter?"

"Yes."

"The time is now 10am. The date is 9th April 2011.

Do you agree I am handing you a form explaining access to the tapes?"

"Yes."

"I am now stopping the recording."

With that, James took the tapes and got David bailed to return in a month pending further enquires.

James made his way back to the police station feeling really pleased; he now actually felt like a real cop. Although, at times, he had wondered why he had chosen to be a cop; James had thought about quitting. It was a very tough learning curve and it not always easy to deal with what you had seen whilst on duty. You had your good and your bad days, just like any job.

Chapter Seventeen – Wet Start

James had been offered some overtime on one of his days off, which fitted in well with Lauren having a girls' night out with Tracy and co.

With his new BMW to pay for, the overtime would come in handy. James had been asked to do some plain clothes burglary patrols as overtime in Otherton. The area had suffered a recent spate of burglaries, mainly in either the late afternoon or overnight. James had been instructed to patrol with the NPT, which consisted of some PCSOs and specials.

However, it was raining very hard tonight, so "PC rain" would probably keep any potential burglars indoors. As criminals always seemed to hate getting either wet or cold, the level of crime would drop on a wet or very cold night. The NPT Inspector had told James via an email what he needed to do and whom he was working with.

The funny part of plain clothes was the need to wear a big coat to cover the stab vest and arrest equipment whilst still looking incognito. Although, on a very wet night like this, James wondered how strange they would look walking around in pairs in the pouring rain.

The first hour was not too bad, but after that, the cold and damp started to seep through. After a further hour, both he and the special were ready for a cup of tea in the warm station before going out again. At least James was getting time and a half for this, unlike the poor special who had volunteered to come out on a wet Thursday night, before going back to his full-time job in a bank in just a few hours' time. "He must be totally mad or very dedicated," thought James.

James sent a couple of texts to Lauren, who enjoyed taunting him about being wet and cold when she was warm and dry.

By 2am, James was thoroughly soaked; not one item of clothing was actually dry. He was about as wet as if he had jumped fully clothed into a swimming pool. Thankfully, he had a change of clothes in his locker at the station. They had not seen anything suspicious as they walked around the hotspot area at least four times, thanks to PC Rain. James could not wait to get home and into a nice hot shower.

The next day, James and Lauren had planned to go off for a few days away in the Lake District. James wanted to use his car as he had yet to take it for a longer run since getting it two weeks ago.

On the motorway, the traffic was quite bad and mainly stop-start all the way. James had only just managed to get everything into the boot and was amazed that the boot of a so-called "bigger" car was not that much bigger than that of his old Fiesta.

James had never really asked Lauren about her ex-husband and she had kept quiet. He knew about the break-up, but nothing to do with how they had got together and what had happened.

Stuck in a car for a few hours, he just came out with it.

"How did you and Dean meet then?"

Lauren, for once, was actually quite willing to talk about Dean.

She met him when she was working in a posh nightclub before she was accepted into the police. Like James, Dean was not the usual type of bloke that she went for.

Lauren started the story, but told James nobody at the station knew about her previous occupation; not that it was that bad. However, she always thought other cops might not take her seriously if they knew.

130

She had always told them she had worked in a shop as opposed to being a nightclub waitress and hostess.

"Lauren, you're late." Peter's half smile let Lauren know that she wasn't fired. At least not yet, anyway.

"I'm only a few seconds late. Besides, in a lot of locations it would be called fashionably late."

"Not at the Pink Coconut. Tables six and seven haven't had their orders taken yet. Beware, they look like potential players." Said Peter

"Aren't they all?" Lauren said over her shoulder as she tied her apron around her slim waist. To Lauren, a player was the exact type of man who had left her over a year ago.

Soon after finishing school, Lauren had applied for the waitress position at the Coconut nightclub, where she could be constantly reminded of the kind of guy she never wanted to become involved with again.

Peter and Lauren had become fast friends right from the start. Peter had a lot of insightful wisdom that Lauren soaked up like a sponge. Together, they had a lot of fun coming up with the many different types of player to suit the types of men who frequented the nightclub. There were the fruit players, kind of sweet but still only after one thing. Then there were the corn players, who told corny jokes as come-ons, the nut players, who were just plain nuts, and the bran players, who were simply too old to be trolling for young women.

Occasionally, she would run into an actual fruitcake.

She made her way over to the first table where two men sat in their casual suit jackets with crew neck tee shirts underneath. Miami Vice was years ago, yet this look never seemed to go out of style. They were staring out into the crowd of dancers as if they were looking for someone in particular.

"Hi there, what can I get you?" she asked in her usual polite voice, raised enough to be heard over the music.

Both of their heads turned at the same time and smiles lit up their faces. Lauren knew immediately that these were typical male customers. They would no doubt try to pick her up, and when she 'gracefully' let them down, they would move on to other potential conquests. They would eventually find a girl who was willing to dance, and if they were lucky, they would get lucky. It made Lauren sick, and that sick feeling was exactly what she thought she needed to avoid getting into another relationship disaster.

"Don't you look hot?" the one on the left said, letting his eyes wander her body.

"Wow, she's hotter than any girl here," the other one said to his friend, but with his eyes on Lauren.

Lauren said, "I can hear you, you know. You two should be careful. You might dehydrate from all that drooling. Say, I have an idea; why don't I get you something to drink?"

She kept her casual smile as she issued the sarcasm.

"Bottle of Beck's for me, honey."

"Same here, baby."

She walked away with their order and gave it to Peter.

"Was I right?" Peter asked.

"On the nose. We need a new kind of player that describes idiots, Peter." Lauren's eyes drifted to the other table she was about to serve. Yep, that is right, two more good-looking men, and undoubtedly players. She picked up the tray with the beers and took it over to the first two idiots.

"Baby, you look good enough to eat!" the 'baby' man said. His friend followed up with, "What time do you get off, honey?"

Never with you mate, Lauren thought to herself. She set the two drinks down and said, "First of all, I'm not on the menu, and secondly, here's a little advice: You can't both try to pick me up at the same time, and more importantly, neither of you should try to pick me up at all."

She turned away from them and walked to the next table. I hope that these two players would not be as blatantly stupid.

"Hi, what can I get for you?" Lauren said in her usual tone.

"How about your number?" the one on the right asked.

Lauren had heard that line so many times it was not even funny. She did notice that the guy on the left shook his head and looked down at the table as if he might be embarrassed by the behaviour of his friend. She replied with her best Essex girl impression: "Um, I think you might have missed the free brochure available at the door, right next to our bouncer. It lists lamest pick-up lines that died with the dinosaurs."

She leaned in closer to the guy and added in her regular voice, "By the way. I've heard 'how about your number' over a thousand times, and so has every other girl. You might want to spice it up a bit." She stood up straight, gave a disapproving look, and said, "What can I get you boys tonight?"

The other person looked up into her eyes and said in a calm, smooth voice, "We'll just have two bottles of lager, thanks."

Lauren was caught off guard at the easiness of this one's voice and the way his dark eyes transfixed her. Lauren's guard was always up because it had to be, but with this guy, she immediately felt that she didn't need to be processing a comeback. She turned and walked to the bar.

"Two bottles of lager," she told Peter.

Peter was wiping out a glass and looking beyond her head. "More players?"

"Yeah. Well, one of them is. The other one may not be."

"Would that be the one who hasn't taken his eyes off you since you left the table?" said Peter.

Her head whirled around to see those sexy dark eyes on her. She looked back at Peter and said with a sigh, "Maybe he is a player."

"You like him," he said with an accusatory tone.

"What?"

"I think you like him."

"That's ridiculous. I do not even know him. He's probably just like all the other men in this joint."

"Hey, that's not nice."

"Except you, Peter." She smiled and took the drinks over to the table.

After she set the drinks down, she looked at the one on the left and asked, "Can I get you anything else?"

"No thanks." His eyes twinkled momentarily, and then he looked down at his beer.

Lauren left the table and headed to another one that had just filled with several girls.

"Damn, she's hot!" Stu said to Dean.

Stu drank a few swallows from his bottle and got up and left. Dean sat there for the next hour and watched the beautiful waitress while he nursed his lager.

Dean overheard her quick-witted comebacks to other male customers, which told him she was intelligent and clever, and not to mention funny. So why was a girl like her working in a place like this?

It was clear to Dean that most of the men who came to this nightclub held a certain assumption of the women they expected to meet. However, Lauren held her own and refused any and all advances, including Stu's. She was the most interesting person he had ever met, and she was gorgeous. Dean was glad Stu convinced him to come here.

"Lauren," Peter said, looking over Lauren's shoulder at Dean, "you have an admirer. He looks like a nice guy."

"I'm sure he's planning his pick-up lines and will ask me what time I get off work, or some other run-of-the-mill idiom designed to tempt me into his bed. He's probably just like all the others," Lauren said.

"A little in love yourself?"

"Come on Peter, you know every guy comes here ready to walk out with anyone who's willing. I'm not the only one they use those stupid lines on. I'm just usually the first. It's my duty to all humanity to put them down quickly and harshly."

"Well, your admirer doesn't fit the bill. He looks very out of place and uncomfortable, and certainly doesn't act like a player. You should give him a chance, Lauren."

"I don't give chances anymore."

"How long has it been, Lauren?"

She looked away from Peter's concerned glare. She knew what he was trying to do, what he was suggesting, and she knew he had an amazing sense of intuition about people in general. He would not push her toward a loser.

"I only want you to be happy, Lauren. Give this guy a chance."

Give this guy a chance to stomp on my heart, yeah right. Still, she had been watching the guy in question out of the corner of her eye for the last hour. She watched as he turned down several girls who had approached him, only to have his attentions return to her. There was an interesting look in his eyes; it was one that she could not quite decipher or understand, but it was certainly not like the other men in the club. No, this guy was definitely different, respectful almost. Maybe Peter could sense that too.

Lauren walked over to his table, determined to play fair. This would be a fun experiment, and no doubt he would fail just like every other guy that ever came to the Coconut. However, what if he wasn't like every other guy? This is just to shut Peter up, nothing else.

"Can I get you anything else?" Lauren said as she cleared the bottles away

"No, I'm good," said Dean. He looked at her quickly and then back down at his drink.

"Where's your friend?"

Dean motioned in Stu's direction.

Lauren turned her head to look. Then she looked back at him.

"Why aren't you out there enjoying the evening?"

"There isn't anyone that interests me out there."

Her brows scrunched together in heavy contemplation. It was obvious that he liked her but was not using the usual chat up lines. It was more like bait. She would have to step it up a notch if she was going to win the bet.

"Do you mind if I sit down for a minute? I'm Lauren, by the way."

Dean lost his breath somewhere between his toes and nose as he nodded his approval. He took a sip of his beer and inhaled slowly, trying to get a hold of his excitement. Her musky floral scent hit his nose, stealing his breath once again.

"I'm Dean." He did not know what else to add, so he said nothing.

His silence made Lauren feel uneasy and as if she was intruding. Normally she would have excused herself, but she wanted to go home early so she pressed on.

"Dean, you don't seem like the kind of guy I see here on a regular basis."

"I don't do the club thing. Stu, my friend, pulled me along tonight."

"Well, if you don't frequent clubs, what do you usually do with your weekends?"

Dean took another sip and looked down at the table.

"Being a trainee doctor, I don't seem to have that much time. I'm usually over at my mum's, helping her. Ever since my father died two years ago, she's never been the same."

Dean cleared his throat and attempted a subject change.

"What about you, Lauren? Do you like working in a place like this?"

"A place like this?" Her eyes narrowed slightly.

He realised how offensive his question could be taken, so he reiterated with, "What I mean to say is, you seem like a very intelligent

137

girl, and from what I'm seeing, there seems to be a shortage of brainwaves flowing through this place, both male and female. Anyway, you kind of stand out, as if you don't belong here."

Should she tell him her ambition and what she really wanted to do, or would it scare him off?

"I want to be a police officer. I am just doing this whilst I wait to apply on the next recruitment drive."

Dean reached across the table and laid his hand over hers.

"Oh wow, that sounds like a good career choice, and with your quick-witted nature I am sure you will do well"

She looked at him with her mouth half open, not knowing what to say or how to react. She had not been in a situation like this where the guy came across as sensitive, caring and understanding. Then again, she was constantly surrounded by morons who viewed her as a piece of meat.

Their silent staring match was interrupted by Stu.

"Hey, Dean, I'm heading out. See you later." Stu winked and pulled the short blonde girl closer to his side. Neither Dean nor Lauren acknowledged him. "Hey." He snapped his fingers in front of Dean's face "Get a room, you two." With that, he left with the female he had picked up.

Dean cleared his throat and looked down at their clasped hands on the table. He looked up at Lauren, who had closed her mouth and was now smiling beautifully at him.

"I'm sorry, Lauren. I should go." He stood up, pulling out his wallet to pay for the beers. He was so close to being able to ask her out, so close, but Stu had to kill the moment. Dean decided right there that he was not going to let her slip away without a fight. He would come some other night and see her again.

She stood up next to him, straightening her apron, and looked up at his comforting smile. It really had been a long time since she felt the unmistakable jolt of exhilaration and expectation. It felt very good. She watched him open his mouth as if he was about to say something.

"Would you want to go out with me sometime?" The question loomed in the air.

"Sure," said Lauren, trying not to sound too pleased.

Dean handed Lauren a card from his wallet and she accepted it with a smile. Then she turned and headed toward Peter, almost skipping with delight. Peter really hoped his instincts were accurate on this one because Lauren deserved a good guy for once.

Lauren and Dean were married one year later. Things were good for the first couple of years, but then they just seemed to drift apart, before Lauren found out that Dean was having an affair.

With that, Lauren seemed to go quiet for a while before saying,

"You know what James? It is time I put the past behind me and got on with life. You really have been a breath of fresh air, and a few years ago I would have called you a geek player!"

James and Lauren both laughed as James put his foot down, with the traffic congestion disappearing as quickly as it had appeared.

PART TWO – THE FUTURE

Five Years Later

James had been a cop for five years now and had already seen quite a few changes. The Human Rights Act had been abolished and replaced with the Bill of Rights; criminals no longer had the upper hand. The litigation culture had been brought to an abrupt end due to legislation and changes in the way people could make claims. The knock-on effect was fewer daft health and safety rules and more common sense.

More police officers now carried a Taser instead of either CS spray or PAVA spray. The riots of 2011 had improved life for young people, with more training and learning opportunities. Cuts and reduction of funding had meant a loss of 16,000 police officers. The service had never been so stretched and expected to do more for less.

James was still very happy with Lauren, and they had moved into a house together. Like most couples, they had their difficulties, but were now engaged to be married later on in the year. Lauren was a sergeant at another police station based in the city centre. She was slightly hesitant about getting married for the second time.

The shift, other than losing Lauren, had also seen Chris transfer to another police force to be closer to his girlfriend. Ian was now the shift's advanced driver and was currently tutoring a new police officer called Lucy, the shift's latest edition. Lucy was in her late twenties and had decided on a career change. She had been a supermarket manager for quite a few years and wanted a change of direction, along with a new challenge. Lucy was proving to be a real asset and had the potential to become a good cop. Another female cop, Caroline, had joined the shift from the city centre to replace Chris. She had not long come back after maternity leave, although currently she only worked the morning and afternoon shifts.

The employment freeze for new cops joining had been lifted with the proviso that anyone applying to be a cop must have been either a PCSO or a special constable for a year. They also had to be competent and have had a recommendation to employ from their full-time inspector. The upshot was that many new officers had greater experience prior to going full-time, and retention of new officers had improved.

James really did enjoy being a cop and was revising hard for his Part 1 OSPRE exam, which was needed as part of the promotion process to enable him to become a sergeant. Lauren had passed her exam in the top 10% last year. James had also recently put in an application for armed response and was waiting to hear back from them.

"Morning, mate." James spun around to see Ian beaming at him.

"Morning."

Ian started telling James another one of his stories; this time, it was that whilst taking his dog for a walk, the dog had run back to him with what looked like a stick in his mouth. The stick had turned out to be a live adder and he had quickly pulled it out of his dog's mouth and thrown it into some bushes.

James half listened, but was pre-occupied with getting paperwork ready for a court appearance later on in the week. The upside was that he would miss a night shift to attend.

It was for a job James had attended six months ago, which involved a driver who had failed to stop and had been drink driving.

At 2am, James and Ian were out in the almost brand new BMW 328i with its turbo charged 4 cylinder engine and 245Bhp, which made it quicker than the old Volvo V70 T5 and later D5.

As they drove towards Otherton, they both spotted a white van with no lights on. They turned round and caught up with the van; as soon as they got behind it, James and Ian knew something was amiss. Having no lights on could mean that it was stolen. Ian activated the blue lights that then lit up the rather dark road. He pressed the siren as he drew up close behind the car, and as soon as the driver heard the noise and probably saw the blue lights, he put his foot down and started to make off.

Initially the BMW had no problems keeping up, but the van started to use some back roads with speed humps and did not slow down for them. The weight of the BMW with all its extra kit meant it could easily scrape and bottom out over the speed bumps, so Ian had to slow down.

James was on the radio giving commentary of the pursuit, and they were authorised to continue. Other police cars made their way to the area to help.

James and Ian could still see the van in the distance before it disappeared round a corner. As they turned the corner, the van was now on its side in the middle of the road. Glass covered the road and sparkled like diamonds as the police car lights hit it.

The driver of the van was in the process of crawling out as James and Ian ran over to see if he was alright. As they helped him out, James could smell alcohol on his breath.

The man looked to be in his teens, with a shaven head and wearing a tracksuit top and jeans. He had emerged out of the van without a scratch on him. He had been very lucky indeed.

James took the male to the side of the road and asked, "Have you had anything to drink tonight, mate?"

The man replied, "Yes, I have had three cans of Stella and a can of Strongbow."

"OK, why did you make off from us then, fella?"

At this point, the man burst into tears and kept saying,

"I am so sorry, I am so sorry, I have been really stupid, don't know why I did it."

Ian came back with the breath box and got the male to blow on it.

After a few seconds, the breathalyser came back with a fail; at 70, he was well over the limit of 35.

James then said, "I am arresting you for driving over the prescribed limit, dangerous driving and failing to stop. You do not have to say anything but it may harm your defence when questioned something you do not mention and later rely on in court. Anything you do say may be given in evidence. Do you understand?"

"Yes, yes," replied the man.

"What is your name and address, fella?"

"Mathew Brown, 56 Bramley Lane, Otherton."

With this, Mathew was handcuffed and placed into the back of the police car, ready for the trip to custody.

The drink driving had already been dealt with at the magistrate's court, but the dangerous driving needed to be heard in court as

Mathew had been found not guilty, even with the evidence from the police car's video camera.

Ian was also due in court with James. James had become quite used to court appearances. The first was very harrowing; James shook like a leaf whilst stuttering away as he was questioned and cross-examined in the witness box.

After briefing, James spent half an hour trawling through various files and making sure everything was completed for a couple of bail backs, as well as his court appearance.

Before getting out on patrol, James was asked to pull in a school visit on road safety. James seemed to have a natural manner with children. Every school visit he had done, the children had been enthralled with his enthusiasm and ability to communicate well at their level.

Lauren was constantly making comments about what a great dad he would make; almost hinting at them having children, James thought. Having kids was not something James had considered. For now, he was more than happy with Lauren, their very cute chocolate brown Cockapoo called Maisy, and of course his job. The dog had been enough of a shock, what with her constant energy and bounding around the house, and presents of dog turds in the lounge or on the stairs and the odd puddle that James had managed to step in. Maisy was Lauren's alternative to having a child, or that is what she had led James to believe.

The minute James had walked out of the school and back to the car and said he was available for jobs, he got a call over the radio about a Mazda MX5 sports car that had been driving dangerously. As James was about half way to the last reported sighting of the Mazda, he was diverted to a call of a single car RTC further down the same road.

On arrival, James found the car in the RTC to be the same one that had been reported driving dangerously.

The driver had been thrown clear, but the passenger was still pinned under the car. With it being a warm spring day, they had decided to have the hood down, but neither of them was wearing any seatbelts.

The MX5 left the left side of the road in a curve. The car had been seen travelling at way above the 60mph speed limit by witnesses. The car had travelled about 50 feet before going into the ditch, which was about six feet deep. The car had turned upside down and snapped several small trees before coming to rest on an up-rooted tree.

The fire brigade and ambulance crews were already at the scene when James arrived. James and the fire brigade went down into the ditch, which had about three inches of water in it, to see if they could help the passenger. He was lying face down. From the middle of his shoulder blades upwards, he was hidden by the car on top of him and pinned against the tree below. The fire crew searched for a pulse, but he was dead. It was now down to the fire crew to get the body out.

The paramedics turned their attention to the driver who was still alive, although in quite a bad way. He had also ended up in the ditch, but on being thrown clear, had landed on a pile of soft mud that broke his fall. He was still in a bad way, but alive at least. By now, Ian and Sergeant Bloor had arrived to survey the scene. Due to the severity and removal of a body, they had used the police cars to block the road and close it off. Ian had brought an almost brand new special, who had been sitting around in the parade room with nothing to do. The special was promptly put to work getting the traffic to turn around with the roadblock in place.

Ian's student officer was out with Caroline today, spending most of the day interviewing two suspects for an assault that the night shift had handed over.

James, Ian and Sergeant Bloor stood at the top of the ditch, whilst the fire crew removed the body. What they could see of the body did not appear to be in too bad shape. The body was wedged tightly between the car and the tree. They thought the man had died of a crushed chest.

The fire crew was having a hard time getting the body out, so they finally tied a line to the car and tied it off so the car could not settle any lower than it already was. Two fire fighters pushed down on the tree trunk and as they got it to move several inches, another fire fighter would pull the body a little further each time.

There was a fire fighter on the right side of the body; another one was on the left side, right beside the legs.

One fire fighter shouted, "He is almost free, one more time should do it."

They pushed down once more, as hard as they could. The fire fighter pulled hard on the shoulders of the body and it came free.

As it came free, the fire fighter pulling said, "Oh my god!"

At the same time, he let the body go, which he had pulled out by the shoulders. The body fell backwards toward another fire fighter.

He looked down as the shoulders came to rest against his legs. What he saw sent a cold chill up James' spine. The body had been decapitated. James turned round to see Ian and Sergeant Bloor had moved away, almost as if they knew what was coming next.

The special directing traffic had been lucky to escape the horrific sight, especially as he had only a few weeks' service under his belt.

This was yet another fatal accident James had attended, where deaths or serious injury may have been prevented if only seatbelts had been worn.

Chapter Two – Suicide Followed by Rape

Greg Shetland was well known to the police; he was, to say the least, a little eccentric and suffered mental health issues. He had been frequently reported to the police for putting a TV facing outwards in his window. He did this so it would "keep bad people away." His house was full of strange contraptions and inventions. James had tried to ask him about them on his last visit after further complaints of the TV in the window.

Greg was in his fifties and his early life had been a mixture of care homes and secure units for people with mental health issues. He was very talented when it came to inventing. Sadly, being so eccentric, nobody could actually understand what he had invented and what it was for. Greg was also suspicious of anyone stealing his ideas; especially aliens, that he thought lived amongst human beings.

On this occasion, the neighbours had rung the police as they had not seen him for two weeks. James went round and could not see any life in the house, which was strange, as Greg rarely ever left the house and all doors and windows were secure.

James radioed through and made the decision to kick the door in. Thankfully, the door was an older wooden door, not one of the more modern and difficult to break UPVC doors. Two good kicks and the door flung open with a crack as part of the doorframe broke away.

As soon as he entered, the smell took him back five years to the first house death he had been called to with Lauren. As he walked into the hall, he looked up and on a single piece of rope; Greg's decomposed body was hanging, just moving slightly in the breeze coming through the front door.

"What a way to go and how very sad," thought James. James had always felt sorry for Greg, living on his own with his mental state, and thought it was almost cruel.

Paramedics were called as a matter of routine and then followed by a doctor to certify death. The obvious decomposition meant he was dead, but procedures had to be followed. Scenes of Crime arrived after the doctor, and finally the undertaker was able to take the body to the morgue for an autopsy. James had to do the usual mountain of paperwork and prepare a file for the coroner. It did look like suicide, but the results of the autopsy and crime scene examination would be needed to back this up.

James was already on edge, as today was the day he would find out if his application for armed response had gone through. He had passed the first stage and been for psychosomatic assessment. This consisted of a whole host of questions, some quite strange and bizarre. This was all to make sure James was mentally fit to carry a firearm. This was followed by a board interview, which was more in-depth than the interview he had to pass when he joined the police service.

He knew it was going to be one of those days, with one load of paperwork to do for the sudden death of Greg. "What next?"

Within moments of those thoughts, James was asked to go to a woman who had reported domestic abuse and marital rape. Domestic violence was something James' force took very seriously, as James remembered the recent training session. On average, every week, two women were killed by a partner or former partner. A woman's current or former partner committed 54% of UK rapes.

James had checked for previous at the house on route, and about four months ago, the police had been called to reports of domestic violence. The woman, a Nasreen Ahktar, greeted James at the door. As she opened it, a smell of spices hit James. Nasreen had a strong Indian accent and James initially found it hard to understand her. He sat down on the sofa whilst a three-year-old girl played in the corner of the living room. Nasreen started to explain what had happened.

Nasreen was originally from Pakistan and had an arranged marriage with her husband Mohammed. She had lived in Britain for just over three years now, and the problems began before she was even married, back in Pakistan.

Her husband, almost from day one, had been very controlling, not allowing her to go out or even speak to anyone outside of the family. During the past three years she had been beaten up about 17 times, and on the last few occasions, had taken photos of the bruises and injuries she had sustained. Each time he would apologise, say it would never happen again, and reassure her things would be better.

Nasreen's husband would often come home and demand sex, asking her to strip off naked and lie on the bed whilst he had sex with her. She did not want to have sex and did not give consent, so this was in effect rape. This again had gone on for the past three years. On the 17th time he had assaulted her, she had decided enough was enough and phoned the police. Cops turned up, but Nasreen decided she did not want to press charges. With this, Mohammed felt betrayed and left her. He went back to live with his parents. That was three months ago, and he was already engaged to another Pakistani woman.

James asked what the reason was for deciding to report it now. Nasreen said that he was constantly ringing her or coming round to see his daughter. He had also told his daughter that she needed a new mummy, as his current mummy was bad. A friend had told her that she needed to tell the police, and also recommended that she speak to Refuge, an organisation dedicated to supporting women and children involved in domestic violence. Being quite new to the UK, she had no idea on her rights or the law, and the Asian community around her had put the blame on her for Mohammed leaving. After speaking to Refuge, they insisted that she really needed to get in contact with the police.

James realised this would be a job for CID. His job now was to take a good statement and all the other basic details so he could pass it on the domestic violence unit and CID. The domestic violence unit would look towards ensuring the safety of Nasreen and her daughter as the first priority. He also did a risk assessment and placed her at high risk due to the circumstances and her husband's violent and obsessive behaviour.

After just over two hours with Nasreen, James had the basics done and decided it would be best not to tell control he had finished the job until the paperwork was complete back at the station, just in case they sent him to something else.

The minute James walked into the parade room at the police station, Sergeant Bloor said, "In here, PC Sowman."

James thought, "Uh oh, what I have done this time?"

Sergeant Bloor was sitting at his desk with a very stern look on his face, making James even more concerned.

"PC Sowman, I need to have a talk to you about something.

It has come to my attention that you will be leaving us soon."

Now James really was worried.

"Seems that armed response have been mad enough to accept you!

Very well done!" A big grin formed on Sergeant Bloor's face

Typical wind-up from the sergeant. James did not mind this time; he was too elated to have found out he had got in.

"Let me know when you have your training date. It will be sad to see you go, although I will not miss the lousy cups of tea you make. You should have been got rid of for that years ago."

"Err thanks sergeant. Wow, really had not expected to get in first time."

It had come as quite a shock and total surprise. The various jobs James had attended to meant he had totally forgotten about the results of his application coming.

CHAPTER THREE – STAG NIGHT

James was off down to London this weekend for his stag do. It was also a combined leaving do before he started training for armed response. Ian, Chris and Sergeant Bloor, along with his best man Steve and several other cops, piled onto the train for the hour's journey into London. They had a hotel booked in Leicester Square, although just a Premier Inn. James had not been to London for years; the last time was with his ex-girlfriend when they had come to watch a West End show, "Miss Saigon", for her birthday.

James had known his best man Steve since the age of five. They went to the same primary and secondary school. Although they never really got on at school, a chance meeting saw them get chatting about computers and they found they had a lot in common. Even more intriguing is that Steve's dad been re-married to the mum of another good friend of his, Adrian, a few years back.

Steve was a good mate and could always be relied upon, even if he did have a tendency to drink a little too much. Like James, he had been to university and studied Computer Science. He was now doing very well as a programmer, earning nearly twice as much as James. He landed on his feet; the work placement in his gap year was so impressed that they offered him a full-time position on graduation and paid his final year fees.

London had not changed; as soon as they got off the train, they were almost hustled into the Underground by the sheer number of people. There were queues, even for the automated tickets, and people were criss-crossing everywhere. The odd person would bump into another as they raced for the various escalators to the tube lines. It was like watching a container full of marbles thrown onto the floor cascading in all directions, some bumping into each other.

Ian had already managed to barge in and get his ticket. He was now staring at the map and scratching his head, trying to work out which tube line they needed for Leicester Square. Chris came up behind him and said, "We need the Northern Line for Leicester Square."

Ian was just about to mutter "Clever clogs," when he remembered that Chris had been at university in London.

The tube was crammed full of people and quite hot, with the mixed smell of perfume and sweaty bodies. Thankfully, only two stops and they would be at Leicester Square. The hotel was just a few hundred metres down the road from the underground station.

They all had twin rooms to keep the costs down, and James was with his best man Steve. The plan was to get changed, go out drinking, and then come back pretty much when they could drink no more. Even after an hour in London, a hot shower was so refreshing after the hot Underground.

They all left the hotel and made their way to Leicester Square, which was full of restaurants and, of course, the cinema that had hosted many film premieres.

Chris again took the lead and said, "I know just the place to go to first."

He took them to the Tiger pub in the Haymarket, which, like everything else in London, was busy. They had the Comedy Store booked for later on, which was not too far away.

The beer started to flow and everyone was quite tipsy and a wee bit hungry, so they piled into the nearest McDonald's for something to eat.

The Comedy Store was a hoot, although some rather rowdy South Africans had to be removed, mainly due to the racist comments they made about a black comedian. Some acts were funny; Steve Gribbin from Liverpool, with his scabrous comedy songs and bizarre observations, had been one of the highlights. His songs had razor sharp lyrics with tunes that ended up getting locked in James' mind and then refusing to leave.

After the Comedy Store, the now rather drunk group of cops and a civilian made their way to Soho under the guidance of Chris, who knew an excellent Chinese restaurant where they could get some food, before going onto a club. All was going really well until James walked straight into a lamppost and sent himself flying backwards onto the pavement.

The lamppost had a textured finish; it had left James with a nasty graze and bump. Ian and Chris took James to the nearest bar to get a plaster. The bar was quite olde worlde, with rustic beams and nautical pictures and objects. It was quite busy and packed full with men.

Ian went to the barman and asked if he had a plaster; the barman obliged, but he only had those bright blue catering plasters. Chris started to look around; he noticed that there was a picture of Noel Coward on the wall, and there was not one woman in the bar. A group of men were eyeing Ian up and down. It hit Chris they were actually in a gay bar and it brought a smile to his face.

Neither Ian nor James had any idea they had been in a gay bar. Chris was very unbothered about it, but the idea of Ian being eyed up by a group of men was priceless banter material.

The groups finally made it to the Chinese restaurant, Y Ming, and were seated. In total, they ordered twenty dishes between them, not far off half the menu. After the meal, everyone piled out and headed onto a club. It was quite a cool night and the air made everyone feel even more intoxicated than they already were, and most were unsteady on their feet. Ian told James to watch out for lampposts.

They tried to get into a club, but were refused due to James' cut, which now looked more as if he had had a fight than been in an altercation with a lamppost. Removing the plaster had actually made it look far worse. Instead of a club, it was a few more beers in a bar before heading back to the hotel.

The next morning, everyone was worse for wear; James' mate Steve had especially gone a nice shade of green and had already been sick twice. They all bypassed a cooked breakfast, fearing it would not stay down for long. Instead of breakfast, a trip to the shops to buy gifts for girlfriends was thought to be a good idea, before heading to the train station.

Ian fell asleep on the train home; his snoring was so loud Chris had to wake him up due to complaints. It had been a good night and James even had an injury to prove it.

Ian then proceeded to tell a funny story about his dad, who was a retired cop.

His dad, having gained his police driving permit at the third attempt, was keen to make a good impression. Just as he was collecting the car keys from the patrol sergeant's office for his first solo "Panda" patrol, he walked smack bang into the superintendent, who was on his way to star in the local amateur 'Gilbert & Sullivan' play.

He wished Ian's dad all the best and hoped he would make a better job of keeping his eyes open once he commenced his patrol. Determined to show him what a fine officer he was becoming, Ian's dad thoroughly checked the vehicle, re-inflating the tyres and topping up the oil and water bottles. Once a quick inspection for damage was completed, he was out on patrol. He decided to go to some of the remote rural areas of his patch that he hadn't seen when assigned foot patrol duties with the other non-driving officers.

Once out into the country lanes, he was congratulating himself on being paid to drive the superb, rear-engined, 850cc Hillman Imp, when he spotted a broken down vehicle up ahead. He pulled in behind and could not believe his good fortune when a head popped out from the nearside of the car, and it was the one and same superintendent. Here was his chance to get back in his good books. Ian's dad asked him if he needed a hand and he said he certainly did. Handing him his car keys, he asked if Ian's dad could get the spare tyre and the jack out from the boot. He did as requested and, the superintendent assuring him he could manage, Ian's dad resumed his patrol.

He continued on his rural patrol, surprised that the radio was so quiet. In those days, only one car known as the Area or 999 car was equipped with a force radio; the rest of the cops had a cumbersome two-set affair tuned to the front office of the police station. Unbeknown to Ian's dad, he had strayed far beyond the limits of the small handheld sets.

About an hour or so later, he returned to the town area and was aware that a rather exasperated station sergeant was hailing his call sign over the radio. He was told in no uncertain terms to return to his previous rendezvous point with the superintendent, with as much haste as was humanly possible. Ian's dad returned to the delights of the countryside and was rather surprised to find the superintendent in exactly the same place he had left him, but now changed into his full theatrical costume!

The superintendent then said, "You blithering idiot. You drove off with my car keys; I have missed the first act!"

Horrified, Ian's dad removed the superintendent's car keys from his pocket and handed them over before he drove off in a cloud of dust, leaving Ian's dad red-faced in his vapour trail.

With the story finished, James, who was quite witty and sharp, said, "So there are two calamity Collins' in the family then, eh?"

All the cops cracked up laughing and Steve looked a bit bemused, as if he had missed something. Steve had not heard the stories of Ian's mistakes.

Three weeks later, James had got through his initial firearms course. Like most of the police training he had been through so far, it had been quite intense at times and required some home study.

The aim of the course was to provide all the necessary skills and theory to allow James to become an authorised firearms officer.

The course was two weeks long and included input on the Glock 17 self-loading pistol, various drills, the law, basic firearms tactics, target identification, and containments. Some time was also spent in the simulation gallery, where James had to react to incidents and apply the law to those incidents in as near to real life as could be achieved in a simulator.

A lot of time was also spent on the ranges learning shooting skills and weapon handling. The course structure was designed so that even officers with no experience of firearms would, by the end of the course, be able to complete a shooting test and be competent in the tactical use of police firearms.

James enjoyed the course, and his previous firearms experience during his time in the TA helped immensely as he understood the basic marksmanship principles and weapon handling.

"1. The position and hold must be firm enough to support the weapon. The weapon should be firmly supported with elbows locked in place. The weapon should be relaxedly held, using the natural support of the body.

2. The weapon must be held upright and pointed naturally at the target without undue physical effort. The weapon should point naturally towards the target, being held into place by natural bone support, not by tension of the arm muscles. This will result in a poor and unsteady aim.

3. Sight alignment (aiming) must be correct. The foresight must be in the centre of rear sight aperture, with the target in the middle of the rear sight aperture, forming a straight line from the eye, through the sights, and onto the target.

4. The shot must be released and followed through without disturbing the position. Breathing should be controlled, and can be held if necessary to prevent vertical movement of the body that results from inhalation and exhalation. When pulling the trigger, gentle pressure should slowly be increased until the final pressure is exerted to fire the weapon. Although the recoil caused by the firing will cause the weapon to move, it will return to point naturally at the target. Pause momentarily after firing, before releasing pressure and reloading the weapon."

When he joined the TA, he had always wanted to try to join the SAS, especially after reading several SAS books by Chris Ryan and Andy

McNab. In many ways, they were his inspiration to consider a career in the Army.

With the basic firearms course out of the way, the next course almost back-to-back was the Armed Response Course.

This course looked at other firearms and consisted of a one-week Heckler and Koch MP5 Carbine course. Like the Glock 17, the MP5 is the preferred weapon of both Special Forces and law enforcement agencies across the world. After the MP5 course, this was followed by an intensive three-week ARV course. Again, this was a mixture of shooting on the range and real-life scenarios when James had to make quick decisions to unfolding events. The course had to be strictly assessed and one officer was removed halfway through the course for failing to make the grade.

As well as the shooting and scenarios side of the ARV course, they covered aspects such as team building, vehicle deployments, building containments and firearm make-safes to an advanced level. James did find it very exciting, as well as physically and mentally demanding.

The final course James had to do to complete his training was the advanced driving course, which would mean he could drive the higher powered Focus STs, BMWs and Range Rovers the force had, as well as being able to pursue vehicles.

In some ways, Lauren was a bit jealous as she had yet to do her advanced driving course, even though she had been on the waiting list for the past 18 months. However, as a response sergeant drove a desk more than being out on the beat, Lauren being trained to a higher level was not deemed essential.

With the wedding only months away, the courses had been a nice distraction for James as he had been able to avoid the various trips to florists and cake decorators. That duty had ended up being done by both his and Lauren's mum, taking it in turns.

The costs were mounting and the bank account was becoming empty. James being James, he did not complain as he knew how much Lauren was looking forward to the wedding.

Chapter Four – Bridal Shopping

Lauren was in the bridal shop having a final fitting for her wedding dress. She had gone for a simple but elegant white design that showed off her curves and figure to good effect. As the dressmaker in the dress shop made final adjustments, Lauren looked out into the rather wet and gloomy world through the shop window and remembered her holiday in Majorca with James last year.

Lauren sighed and stared off into the distance across the pier, smiling at the thought of marrying James.

"Hello," a soft voice said from behind Lauren.

Lauren smiled and turned her head to look at James.

"What are you thinking about?" James asked, taking a seat beside her.

"Us."

"Really?"

"Yeah, really," Lauren told him, picking up his hand and playing with his fingers.

"What about us?" James asked, leaning over so he could lift her chin up with his hand.

"Hmm?"

James sighed but kissed Lauren back, wrapping his arms around her waist and pulling her down on top of him. Lauren grinned and kissed his cheek, then along his jaw, until she came to the exposed part of his neck, before planting kisses along it.

"Lauren," James moaned.

"I love you," Lauren told him, pulling away.

"I love you, too," he murmured.

Lauren smiled and looked at him, tracing every part of his face, before leaning in and softly kissing him once more.

"Sweetheart, I love you. But now is not the time to be playing games," James said with an amused grin on his face.

"Aw, come on!" she cried, laughing.

He grinned and leaped to his feet. Then he leaned down and picked her up, so that she was cradled in his arms.

"Get ready," James whispered in Lauren's ear.

She laughed and let out a squeal when he jumped head first into the sea.

"James!" Lauren shouted before she went into the water.

She felt a pair of arms wrap securely around her before pulling her to the surface. Lauren smiled and wrapped her arms around his neck, pulling herself closer to him.

"I love you," James said, brushing Lauren's hair out of her face.

"I love you too," Lauren told him, smiling.

James leaned down and kissed her again before dragging them both under water.

Lauren grinned and pushed him away so that she could swim off without him realising. Lauren swam farther away from him, hoping he would not notice, but when does James ever not notice? Lauren smiled when she felt him grab her foot, before yanking her backwards so that she was back in his arms. She grinned at James under the water and saw him smile back. James shot to the surface, still keeping Lauren in is arms.

"Cold?" James asked, holding Lauren tightly.

"No," she replied, leaning her head against his chest.

"You should be. This water is freezing."

"Not to me."

He sighed and held her tight. Lauren wanted him to hold her. She felt safe in his arms.

She felt a slight prick from a pin touching her shoulder, and her sister shouted, "Wakey, wakey, Lauren, you seem a million miles away."

Lauren was back in the bridal shop with a big smile on her face. She hoped this time everything would be fine. James had become her rock and she would be totally lost without him.

"All done," said the women adjusting Lauren dress.

"You look lovely sweetheart," said Lauren's mum.

Lauren went off and changed back into her clothes, whilst her sister Helena tried on her bridesmaid dress. Forever the exhibitionist, Helena decided she would show off the underwear Lauren had bought her to go with her dress. It was an expensive purple Agent Provocateur bra with high cut purple knickers and a suspender belt. Like Lauren, Helena had a very slender figure, but was slightly taller with longer legs.

Helena decided to parade around the fitting room and do her best pole dancing impression on a pillar in the changing room area. She swished her long brunette hair about whilst kicking her legs into the air and trying to do the splits. Only she ended up on her bottom, tripping over her heels and putting a ladder in her brand new stockings. One thing Helena had still not mastered was walking in heels; she blamed her much-too-long legs for this.

Lauren's mum gave a disapproving look as Helena performed. Lauren just laughed it off.

Helena was four years younger than Lauren. She was a real girly girl, as opposed to Lauren, who was more of a tomboy (although Lauren realised that being a bit more feminine looking on occasions got her more attention). Helena hated wearing trousers and never went out without make-up on.

Helena lacked Lauren's confidence and, for such an attractive woman, found it difficult to get a boyfriend. She had been more dedicated to her studies and done better academically than Lauren. She was now a primary school teacher in quite a posh private school. Lauren and Helena had always got on really well. Lauren had always being there when Helena needed her.

With Helena's dress tried on and adjusted, the next stop was the florist. There was so much to do for the wedding, which was just weeks away.

Meanwhile, James was on his first shift as an Armed Response officer and had just been called out to his first job.

A primary school teacher decided to go into her classroom on Saturday afternoon to do some work. She had parked out front and opened the front door to the school. As she went into the building, she heard some noises and saw a broken window in the office door, which made her suspicious. She quickly left the building and dialled 999.

James responded along with John, his new partner. They met the frightened teacher just down the street from the school. She passed them her school keys and they proceeded to the building. The school was an old Victorian building with real character.

James unlocked the front door and entered. There was a hall running straight ahead of them and one running at a right angle to their left.

The school office was at the inside corner of the halls' intersection, straight ahead and to their left. James and John both pulled out their tasers and approached the office door. They searched the office and found it had been ransacked, but nobody was there now.

They then heard a noise farther down the hall. The way the school was made, it had two hallways that ran its whole length, with classrooms to their outsides and classrooms between them. The sounds seemed to be coming from the rooms that were between the two hallways. John went down the hallway they were in and James ran around to the opposite hall.

He approached the noise as quickly but as quietly as he could. He came to the library, which had double doors that entered both halls. The top half of both doors was glass. James saw two teenagers in the room, which had been vandalised. James was squatting so that he could just look into the window. Both teenagers were looking at the door to the opposite hallway. They must have heard John approaching. James reached up with his left hand and pushed on the doors, but they were still locked.

He ducked as the two turned towards the door he was crouching beside; the teenagers then came over and tried to open the door. When they tried to open the door, James jumped to his feet and, taser still in hand, pointed it against the glass half an inch from the face of the teenager closest to him.

At the same time, James yelled, "You are under arrest!" as loudly as he could.

They both froze. John then came into the library and covered them with his taser while James came around. James handcuffed one then

166

John handcuffed the other. Both teenagers were then searched and taken to the police car before being placed in the back of it. One was an 18-year-old male known to the police for car crime and theft, and the other was a 17-year-old who had never been arrested or even in trouble with the police. They said they had vandalised the school just to have something to do.

John had been a police officer for six years after having spent six years in the Army. He was on the intake before James and had made quite a name for himself as a good "thief taker." John had a very soft Scottish accent. Originally he was from Glasgow, and had moved south when he joined the Army. John was not very tall but was well-built and could handle himself very well indeed. Years spent dealing with drunken soldiers in the Royal Military Police had taught him a ot. John was very blunt and serious, almost the polar opposite to Ian from James' old shift.

John did have a bit of a chuckle when James told him the story of Sergeant Bloor being assaulted last year. Sergeant Bloor was patrolling alone on the nightshift. Whilst arresting a drunk, he had been assaulted. Thankfully he was not badly hurt; just a minor bruise. The funny part was that the offender had been a one-legged man who, during the scuffle, had taken off his artificial leg and hit the sergeant over the head with it. Not your normal method of assault! The sergeant had endured months of banter for that one, including having the leg off a dummy usually found in a shop window put in an evidence bag and placed on his desk.

The second call of the shift came in of a train having hit a person just north of the city centre.

John hit the blue lights and made quick progress. On arrival, they found a freight train had hit a female in her twenties. British Transport Police were on their way, but the nearest unit was about 40 miles from them.

The train driver, still quite shaken, said that the woman was lying down between the tracks when he first saw her. There was no way to stop the train before hitting her. The train had travelled another half a mile before being able to come to a full stop. A train of this size could take up to a mile to stop, the train driver said.

The body was in bad shape and the woman was pronounced dead at the scene. British Transport Police came out to do the crime scene investigation, which included taking pictures of the scene, interviewing all parties involved, and taking measurements. A doctor had come to the scene, pronounced the woman dead, and then released the body to the undertakers, who transported it to the morgue.

James and John were given the task of reporting the death to the next of kin once they had found out who the woman was. They went through the personal belongings that were on the body and found her identification. She was a university student by the name of Samantha Jones.

With this information, they could do the notification of the next of kin. John suggested to James that he give the parents of the woman a call first and ask that they come and speak to them. It was important to do so before any media reports were released, so that the next of kin would not hear about it on the news first.

James called the number he had found for the family and a woman answered the phone. James identified himself and told her that he needed to come by her house to talk to her. She asked James what it was in reference to and he told her that it was about her daughter. James just told her that he would like to talk to her about it face-to-face. She agreed and gave James the address. Next of kin notification was never an easy task, and James thankfully had not had to do many in the past five years.

James remembers Lauren telling him on his first that people react in many different ways to the news of a tragedy like this. "Some react in anger at the person who informs them, others fall apart, and still others act almost like nothing has happened. We all have different ways of dealing with grief and emotion."

James walked up to the door and knocked. The father and mother both came to the door. James introduced himself and then introduced John, who was with him. They invited James and John in and they all sat down in the living room. James took a deep breath and said, "There has been an accident involving your daughter."

The father looked at him and asked, "Is my daughter dead?"

James answered, "Yes, I am so sorry for your loss. Is there anything we can do?"

James tried to explain what had happened, but the mother kept denying that it could possibly be her daughter. The father just sat there and nodded his head in agreement. John asked if there was anyone they could call. Again, the mother just kept repeating over and over again that it was not her daughter. James tried to speak to the father, but he was looking at the floor, still nodding his head.

James gave the mother his card with his name and contact number, and told her that she could call him in the morning if she had any questions. James and John quietly got up and left.

It all seemed kind of surreal somehow to James. They had come to tell them that their daughter was dead, and then just left them in shock. However, what else could he have done? It is one of the most helpless feelings James had ever had, as there was nothing he could say to lessen the pain or shock.

The autopsy showed that Samantha had died of massive internal injuries. It also showed that she was killed instantly from multiple injuries when the train hit her. No illegal drugs were found in her system. She had simply laid down on the tracks and waited for a train to come. There was no reason for her to take her own life. Samantha had a bright future ahead of her; she was doing well at university. Her parents were devastated; they would probably never get over the shock. They had been in touch with James and thanked him for his sensitivity. James and John even attended the funeral at the request of the parents.

CHAPTER FIVE – ROBBERY AND DEMENTIA

At 4am, just as things were starting to slow down, James and John had a call to a pub that was being burgled. The pub, called The Lord Nelson, was on the far side of Otherton, but only a 5 minutes' drive with the blue lights on. On this shift, they had spent more time on blue lights than not. So far, they had used over half a tank of fuel. On arrival at The Lord Nelson, James jumped out and climbed over a fence whilst John went round the front.

James climbed through the smashed window and made his way into the pub. As soon as he got in, he found the proprietor at the bottom of the stairs in the hall. He told James that the offenders had already left. Anxious to get after them, James took some basic details. The proprietor told James that he had held the door to his flat above the pub shut whilst burglars tried to smash the door in. After a while, the burglars had given up and fled empty-handed. The proprietor then showed James the crowbar and torch they had left behind.

"Scenes of crime may be able to get some evidence off them," said James.

With basic details collected and uniform on the scene to get a witness statement, James and John went on an area search, but a report of a second pub burglary quickly came in. This was only just down the road from the Nelson and too much of a coincidence not to be the same offenders, thought James. Once again, they sped off, and within a couple of minutes, they were at the Horse and Hound pub. On arrival, they saw that a window had been smashed, and just as James was about to enter, John shouted and ran into the pub car park at the rear, closely followed by James.

In the car park, a black VW Golf was revving its engine and spinning its wheels, throwing up grey smoke, before heading towards John and trying to make a good getaway. As the car screeched past John, he managed to smash the passenger window with his baton before they escaped.

The registration number came back as a black VW Golf, which had been stolen earlier from a house on the other side of the city.

James and John ran to their car and radioed in all the details on the burglars whilst they tried to re-locate the car. They tried the main roads first, but no sign. They then doubled back round the housing estate and locally-known hiding places, but again to no avail. It was a total loss, which frustrated John especially as he had seen them and had been only 60 seconds from being able to grab them.

"Never mind, John. I am sure we will get them another day. Maybe forensics will get something off the crowbar or torch?"

"Yeah, you're right. It's just so frustrating; I nearly had them. It would have been a good collar."

The rest of the night was pretty much uneventful. James and John pulled a couple of suspicious cars and gave one driver a ticket for using a mobile phone behind the wheel.

It was 6:30am and they were just about to head back to base for the end of the shift when they got a call of a burglary at a posh mansion on the outskirts of Ollerton. The details were sketchy as to whether the burglary was in progress or had just been found. On arrival, an old woman, who said she had just been burgled, greeted them. The house looked pristine, and James and John wondered what she was talking about. She took them to the safe in the bedroom, saying,

"Right this way, young men." Once inside, she showed James about £250,000 worth of jewellery; diamonds, rubies, gold, even a signed invitation to the Queen's tea party.

She then ordered James to take it all away as it was fake. She continued to say that the robbers took all her real stuff and substituted it for this fake jewellery, and that she wanted it all getting rid of. James agreed and knew that something was not quite right with her. He asked if she had any family who could come and help them take it all away as it was too much for them to carry.

She promptly passed the number for her son. He explained in a sleepy voice on the phone to James that, since her husband had died, she just kept slipping away and the dementia was getting worse. They had tried to get her into a home but she had flatly refused. With that, James said to the old woman that they would come back to collect everything later, but for now they would keep it in her safe. John went and locked the safe whilst James checked that the rest of the house was secure, before they both left and resumed.

On the way back, John started talking about his time growing up in Glasgow and his brush with the law as a teenager.

It was mid-afternoon on a nice Spring day; John had just finished college classes for the day when he decided to visit a mate to see if he could pick up some cannabis. He headed over to her place; she was this hippy chick with an apartment on one of the top floors of a 15-story high rise near the centre of Glasgow. They ended up chatting about mundane topics, smoked a joint, and then sampled a little bit of pressed hash.

John was hovering about when his friend stashed the cannabis inside of his baggy zip-up sweater, and then he left her apartment. It took an age for the lift to arrive. As John stood there, he heard someone's deadbolt unlatch; a nearby door opened and this bald guy poked his head out, looked around, saw John, and then shut his door. John thought it was strange at the time, but didn't think much of it. The lift arrived and he got in, pressing "G" for ground and then heading to his car to start the drive home.

As he arrived on the ground floor lobby and stepped out, he saw two uniformed police officers standing around with their backs to the elevators, appearing to be guarding the front door. At this point, John made the quick decision to avoid a confrontation and take a right out of the lift area so he could head out the back entrance of the building. No sooner did John make this decision, than one of the uniformed officers turned around and saw him. As he kept walking towards the back entrance, he heard a loud stern voice that almost made him crap himself. "Excuse me, sir".

John turned around to see this giant of an officer, who had to have been at least 6'2", if not taller. As he walked over to where John was standing, John felt the cannabis that was hidden inside his jumper. It felt like 100+ kg. Not only did it feel heavy, it was also about to slip out from under his jumper. John tried to move his arm to stop it from falling, but the worst thing that could have happened... happened. The bag rustled under his jumper and the officer looked down at where the noise was coming from. Quick thinking on John's part knew he had to distract the officer somehow from the noise, so he asked,

"What can I do for ya, officer?"

The officer replied in a stern voice, "You match a description we have been given. Would you mind talking to us for a minute?"

John replied in the calmest voice he could muster, "Sure."

At this point, John was thinking about how he was going to explain to his family how their son had been arrested with a quarter pound of cannabis. He was hoping the officer would not notice his red eyes, nor the smell coming from the bag under his jumper.

The officer stated again, "You match a description. Could you tell me which floor and which occupant's suite you are coming from?"

Now John knew something was up, because he was a unique-looking individual, and police officers don't just hang around in the lobby of apartment buildings questioning people who come out of the lift, so he lied and said,

"I just dropped by to visit my friend Kyle on the seventh floor."

Of course, he knew no one on the seventh floor, nor did he know anyone named Kyle, but the officer seemed to buy it. After a couple more questions about whether he saw anyone else in the lift, the officer asked what John's name was. John lied again and was both thankful and lucky that the officer did not ask for any ID. After about 5-10 minutes, he was satisfied that John was not the "suspect" they were looking for and told him to carry on his way. John had made a lucky escape that could have changed his life forever. With this close shave, John made the decision to quit college and join the army to get away from the bad influence Glasgow had on him.

CHAPTER SIX – THE BIG DAY

It was Lauren's and James's wedding day, Lauren's mum was doing her usual fussing around much to Lauren's annoyance, even though she was used to her mum being overly fussy.

"This is it, honey, don't forget. This is your big day."

"It's okay, Mum, I get that." thanks, I really needed you to make me more of a gibbering nervous wreck than I already was.

"Just let me smooth the back of your dress."

"My dress is fine, go sit in the church." Lauren answered.

"And your tiara..."

"Will — you — please — go — sit — in — the — church!"

"Ahh, sweetie." You look just beautiful!" said her mum

"Gillian, will you darn well do what your daughter is asking you to do?" Lauren's dad growled. "She's going to pass out from pure terror any second."

He grabbed Lauren's trembling arm and glared at his wife, who nodded, smiled and scuttled into the cool dimness of the church on her three-inch peacock blue heels.

Lauren took a deep breath. If this was bridal nerves, then she had a near-fatal case. She hadn't expected to. All these years she had never dreamed of getting married a second time.

Lauren's mum had always fussed about Lauren and her sister Helena. She had done a good job those as both Lauren and her sister had turned out well. Lauren's mum still hated Lauren being a Police Officer; she always worried about something bad happening to her.

Now, she was about to marry James Sowman, who had been her student and she had known him for five years. However, she still felt more like she was lined up on a hospital trolley waiting for major surgery. In real life, she had never been a great success at the big occasions

"Ready?" her father asked.

"Give me another five seconds."

Her sister, Helena, was looking stunning this afternoon in a lilac satin dress that set off her brunette hair and green eye. She instructed to Lauren. "Drop your shoulders.. Lift your chin."

"James's waiting for you," Helena added softly.

"Yes. He is. Okay. Let us do this. Dad?" She held his arm more tightly.

The aisle of the church had not seemed so long since Lauren during rehearsals. As the organ groaned into life, James turned to gaze at her down the length of worn red carpet. He was miles away, but Lauren could see the usual uplifting smile that had always reassured Lauren.

Lauren's heart beat faster; it was beating so hard she could feel her chest vibrate.

Friends and relatives crammed the church. Dozens of pairs of eyes locked on her face. Sentimental women sniffed into their handkerchiefs. Fidgety males cleared their throats. A little grouchy three year old said loudly, "I wanna go home!"

Yeah, little one, can I come with you? Thought Lauren

All of this form getting to know someone by sitting next to them in a police car for nine-hour shifts. Learning to rely on them and be your back you up when things got sticky.

"I want to marry you," James said, on their fourth date.

Lauren had just taken it as another one of James's jokes to make her feel more confident.

"James —!"

"I'm not asking you. Not yet." He'd grinned and her stomach had dropped like an elevator filled with wild butterflies, around fifty floors. She had not known it was possible to fall for a man this fast and this hard, to feel this right and this confident. "I'm just giving you fair warning of my intentions," he'd said with a small laugh.

"I said I wanna go home!" the four three old yelled.

A woman whispered at him, pulled him up onto her hip and clattered out of the church through a side door. Rattled by the incident as if she needed yet another reason to be rattled! Lauren tripped on the floor-length front of her silver-white satin gown. She heard a ripping sound. Her father said, "Whoa, Lauren!" and the congregation gave a collective gasp.

James started to get nervous and took a step forward. Without turning around, Helena hissed at Lauren. "It's okay. It's just the tulle. The underskirt. I can tell by the sound of it. Don't catch your toe in the tear."

"I'll try. What made me think I could do this?"

James kept trying not to grin. He did not take his eyes from her face. Lauren tried to gain some support from the steadiness of his smile, but she could not. She was too busy working out how not to catch that toe on what she feared must be a gaping tear.

The church aisle stretched out a further six miles or so it felt, but she reached James at last. She wanted a word from him, a reassurance, but

179

nothing came. He took her hands, but they were so shaky and damp that he let them go again almost at once. He ran his fingers down her bare arm, but she hardly felt it.

The vicar moved forward and started his sermon and the marriage of James Alex Sowman and Lauren Maria Reilly.

With the service completed both James and Lauren felt relieved and happy. Even the grouchy three year old had stopped being such a grouch and was now waving his arms and smiling away.

They walked out of the church into bright sunshine, which felt like needles in their eyes after the relatively dark and cool church.

Outside lined up with their batons raised was a guard of honour made up of James and Lauren's shift. James felt immensely proud and pleased at the number of work colleagues who had turned out to support him and Lauren.

They passed through the guard of honour with the photographer snapping away as they moved out of the shadow of the church into the very warm sunshine.

The reception was not a lavish affair and was at the pub that James and Lauren met for their very first date. They still went there for meals and drinks and the landlord had offered the pub for free for their reception, knowing full well he would make money on food and drinks.

With it being such a lovely day the beer garden at the rear could also be used. Being such a warm evening was a real blessing. The disco was to be done by the boyfriend of James's sister.

The after reception meal came the usual speeches James's did he usual "errs and umms" as he went through the various thanks.

The best man's speech had everyone in fits of laughter and Steve had done a great job writing it.

"Aw cheers mate...but now I am expected to stand in front of a room full of people and make a witty speech!"

"Ladies and gentlemen, if there's anybody here this afternoon who's feeling nervous, apprehensive and queasy at the thought of what lies ahead, it's probably because you have just got married to James Sowman."

"James was telling me he intended to love and nurture his marriage the same way he does with his beloved football. He says he is going in fully committed, plans to score every week, change ends at half time and play half the season away from home. Funny that, because if he does, Lauren reckons it's a sure fire way of getting a serious groin injury."

"I know it's traditional for the best man to wax lyrical about the number of ex-girlfriends the groom has had, but I don't want to get into all that. Frankly, I find such macho male posturing vulgar and offensive to the bride. Suffice to say James 69 turned out to be his lucky number."

"I met James at school when he was sitting in the corner of the playground crying after a girl had pulled his shorts down, obviously a shape of things to come. Although I hear now it is the boys in blue who want to pull his trousers down."

"All I left to say is thank everyone for attending the wedding of the year, and remind you not to drink and drive especially the cops present!"

"Oh and finally I have some gifts to give out to those that matter most and have made this wedding such a success."

CHAPTER SEVEN – HONEYMOON

After a fantastic two week honeymoon in the Dominican Republic, James was back at work. James and Lauren had enjoyed two weeks of hot sunshine, sandy beaches and lazing about all day. The 10-hour flight out there had been quite long, but it had been lovely stepping out into the 30-degree heat. The bus transfer to the hotel, the Gran Bahia Principe Cayo Levantado, was not too bad, although they had to wait an hour for the bus after landing.

The hotel itself was like paradise; it had got many rave reviews and James and Lauren could see why. The resort was lovely and clean; the beach and pool areas were well-kept and spotless. The food was amazing and the view from their room was truly stunning.

Many nights had been spent walking hand-in-hand with the sun setting, just talking and enjoying each other's company. As corny as it sounded, it really was a dream come true for Lauren. After her first husband, she never thought she would find anyone else, let alone anyone better. James really had become the most important part of her life.

Back in the parade room on his first shift back, James got the usual banter and questions about how good Lauren was in bed. Most of the guys on the team knew Lauren through having met up on jobs or training courses.

James just laughed it off and got down to the important business of finding out what action he had missed whilst he was off. He had missed the first fatal shooting in months. The gunman had been caught after a tip-off from the public. This was followed by a dawn raid which saw the team swoop in and arrest him. Then a job that had him in stitches, as well as the rest of the unit, was retold.

The shift had been asked to affect an arrest of a violent rape suspect several hours after it had occurred. With him arrested, they went by to get the victim for an ID parade. She had two children and could not leave, so Alan volunteered to watch the kids while Ady transported the victim to the police station. Thankfully the kids were asleep, so Alan stood on the balcony of the flats looking out into the moonlit night sky. His attention was drawn to some flickering candles on the balcony across the street on another block of three storey flats. Through some mini blinds, Alan could see a man caressing what looked like a naked woman. The view was hazy but clear enough to see what was taking place. Alan watched as he climbed on top and began making love to her. The strange part was that she did not move.

When he finished he got up, covering the woman. He covered her body completely, head to toe, tucking the covers under as if he was wrapping a cadaver. It appeared to Alan that he was watching an actual case of necrophilia, compounded by all the burning candles as a sort of shrine. The man he was watching then lay next to the body and began rubbing her body through the covers. She never moved or showed any signs of response. Alan thought he really was witnessing a case of necrophilia.

Upon Ady's return, he agreed with Alan that the flat needed checking. They knocked on the door and the man asked who it was. When Ady uttered the immortal word, "POLICE," the man inside killed the light and they could hear rummaging around in the flat. Through the frosted front door glass, Alan could see the man moving the body out of sight.

184

They banged louder and ordered him to open the door, otherwise they would kick it in. Just as Ady was getting ready to kick the door in, it opened and they went in. This was a small flat so he could not have hidden the body that quickly. Alan went to the bathroom, but nothing. The shower curtain was closed and Alan was sure she had to be in there. Pulling back the shower curtain, Alan again found nothing. As Alan turned back into the hall, he saw a large pile of clothes that might conceal a body. Fearing the worst, Alan pulled some clothes aside and there she was with a big gash in her side... the inflatable doll the man had been having sex with. He had panicked when Alan and Ady had knocked and could not get the air out quickly enough. He slashed the doll's side to get it down quicker, at the same time making it easier to hide it from the police.

That really was one of the funniest stories James had ever heard. The rest of the shift was in stitches, even though they had heard the story before.

Within an hour of being on patrol, James' honeymoon seemed a lifetime ago as they were sent to various jobs. It was business as usual. The first job they were sent to was a report of a man who had barricaded himself in his house with his girlfriend and refused to come out, saying he would kill both his girlfriend and himself. There had been a standoff for several hours and authorisation had been given for armed response to force entry and arrest the male.

Armed response arrived and parked up around the corner. It was a second floor flat they were going to raid. The male was still shouting out of his window at the police below.

"Any of you fucking pigs come up here, I will do her and any fucking pig that comes close before killing myself."

Initially, armed response intended to be as covert as possible until they broke the door down. They did not want to alert the male to their presence, so went up via a different set of steps on the other side of the block of flats. The flats were typical brick and concrete 1970s and were on a rough housing estate in Beechwood across the city from James' old police station. Armed response did not just have a set area to cover, like a response or beat cop. They could be called anywhere in the city and were based just outside of the city centre, close to the main ring road, for easy access across the city.

The armed response guys geared up in full riot gear and shields; the intention was to take him by force and use the taser if necessary, as opposed to using guns, although they all had their Glock sidearms with them.

James, John, Steve and Ady all made their way round the back and up the back stairs, moving quietly. When they got to the flat, the male was held up and Ady got the enforcer ready to do the door in. James and John had their shields ready to burst in through the door and affect the arrest. Ady signalled one, two, and three with his fingers, before banging on the door with the enforcer. He punched a hole straight through the door but was unable to open it. The male had put a set of drawers in front of the door, preventing easy access. James and John had to make the decision to ditch those shields and crawl through the hole with their tasers drawn.

James went in first and, as he lifted his head up, he could see the male was now holding the female with a knife to her throat. She was screaming for him to let him go.

The male shouted, "Stay back fucking pig or I swear I will do her."

The male stood like an angry bull snorting and growling, stamping his foot as if he would charge at any minute.

James instantly pointed the red dot from the laser on his taser straight at the male's chest.

"Let her go or I will use the taser," said James.

John was now at the side of James and also had his taser aimed on the male's chest.

The male stopped for a moment, unsure of what to do. John knew exactly what he was going to do. He had seen that look many times before, both in the army and later on in the police. He fired his taser and the man instantly dropped the knife and fell to his knees.

John shouted, "Continue to struggle and I will taser you again."

James ran over and kicked the knife away, which slid along the floor before hitting the skirting board with a bang. He grabbed the male's right arm and slapped the cuffs on before quickly slapping them on his other hand.

By now, the rest of the team had joined them and helped move the drawers away from the door before removing the man from the flat. Paramedics were just down the hall, waiting in case anyone was injured. With the male removed, they moved in to check on the female in the flat.

The male by now was starting to struggle and being very abusive, telling them they were all dead and had better watch their backs - the usual bravado they had all seen a hundred times over.

On the way back, John went into another war story as he knew James liked to hear them and could understand, even though he had only been in the Territorial Army, or 'STABs' as the regular soldiers called them.

John was in a Puma helicopter flying out to another target. They were escorted by Lynx helicopters and it was an uneventful flight out to the target. As soon as they got to the target, insurgents became alerted to their presence and started firing. Through night vision goggles, the insurgents could be seen moving into the cover of trees below.

Their target was a Taliban leader and his second-in-command. A local informer had spotted him going into the house that they were about to raid. The Lynx helicopters were there to protect the Puma, but also to take out any escaping vehicles.

The door gunner opened the Puma's door and let rip with his gunfire. Fire from the ground became more intense, and the radio crackled with reports as the pilot shouted that it was now hot and dynamic, meaning they were under fire and had to dodge the bullets.

The OC decided to get the men on the ground as quickly as possible. The Puma became engulfed in dust as it tried to land. He decided on a last minute change, but the pilot realised that a Lynx helicopter was passing right over them. He decided to go up and then down quickly. It came down a bit too quickly and slammed into the ground, before rolling over onto its side. The force of the impact threw men out of the helicopter's side door. It was soon realised that three of the men were trapped under the helicopter.

Those that had escaped quickly regrouped to plan a rescue attempt. One soldier was rescued and quickly tended to by the medics. Flames started to lick around the helicopter's gearbox and two men were still trapped. Try as they might, the other two soldiers could not be shifted. Within moments, flames engulfed the helicopter and rounds from the door-mounted machine gun were soon cooking off along with the whoosh of burning flares. The two trapped men were now unreachable and burnt alive.

John said he could still remember the sight and, more specifically, the smell of burning flesh as if it was yesterday. He lost two good mates that night and it was pretty much the reason he decided to leave the army as could not take any more of the loss and the horror of war. However, John then laughed when he said, "I think I see more horror on a Friday night in custody than I did in the Army." John's way of dealing with anything grim was to just turn it into a joke.

James was almost speechless at that tragic story and, all of a sudden, it was not jealousy he felt but sorrow.

John just brushed it off and got on with the more serious business of ogling what were, in his words, "Two fit women."

Chapter Eight – Dinner for Two

Sitting with James at a candlelit table tucked away in the corner of a small but romantic restaurant had been perfect so far. Tonight's dinner reaffirmed everything Lauren knew in her heart to be true. She and James belonged together. Would tonight be the night she asked James about having a baby? The thought made Lauren nervous; they had only been married a few months. She had broached the subject on several occasions but James had just brushed it off. Lauren had become clucky, and the feeling she wanted to have a baby had become stronger and stronger since she had got married.

"Dinner was delicious." As they walked through the park that ran from Cromford Mill down to the river, the temperature warm and the air humid, James rolled up his sleeves. "So, what have you got to tell me?"

Lauren forced her feet to keep moving. She felt nervous and did not know what to tell James or when to tell him.

"Lauren?"

"Look around you," she said, trying to think of something, anything.

People were out enjoying the park before the sun went down. Jogging, walking hand-in-hand, pushing prams and buggies.

At the sight of a man, woman and baby, an ache started in Lauren's stomach and pulsated outwards. That is what she wanted, a family of her own.

She glanced at James. "So what's next for us, then?" Lauren tried to see if she could get James to start a conversation on babies.

His forehead creased. "Dunno really."

James was too busy watching a group of lads playing football and wanted to go and join in.

"No, it's fine, but are there any little things you could do to make the time together more…"

"Fun?" he suggested. "Memorable? Romantic?"

"All of the above."

"Do you want me to tell you or show you?" he asked.

"Both," smiled Lauren

"OK, both?" He grinned. "A grade 'A' student. Remember?"

She nodded and remembered James as her student officer what seemed like years ago, as they strolled past an ice cream van.

"Let's see." He picked a buttercup from the grass. "I'd start with something a little silly like this." He held the flower under Lauren's chin. "Does she love me?"

James studied it closely. "Very interesting."

She swallowed. "W-w-what does it say?"

"Only that you like butter."

Lauren grinned. "Actually, I love butter. And you."

James handed her the buttercup. "Your turn."

She held the flower under his chin. As a yellow spot reflected on his skin, the warmth of his breath and smell of the aftershave she had bought him for Christmas made her tingle. She glanced up at him. The tenderness of his gaze made her want to stay like this forever.

"So do I or don't I?" James asked.

"You do." Her voice sounded strange, husky. She waited for him to look away. He did not. This was her chance to show James what she really wanted.

Still she hesitated. Scared, excited, unsure.

Do it now, before it is too late, she thought.

She had nothing to lose.

Lauren inhaled sharply and kissed him on the lips. A long, lingering kiss, just like the first kiss in the nightclub all those years ago.

As his arms encircled her, his mouth pressed against hers with such affection and love.

Lauren had a flashback to that first kiss in the nightclub over five years ago.

She could not believe this was happening. Her knees trembled and she splayed her hands on his back, the ridges of muscles beneath her palms.

For months, she had imagined James' kisses, but nothing could have prepared her for the real thing. More satisfying than chocolate, more tempting than a bottle of wine. Her heart fluttered. Her pulse skittered. Sensations rippled. Angling his head, he deepened the kiss. A kiss that hinted of things to come. Lauren couldn't wait. She leaned into him, wanting more, so much more...

Then a moment later, Lauren was back in the park, kissing James.

Something nudged between them. Something hard...

"James?" Lauren muttered, not removing her lips from his.

He glanced down. A dog, a black Labrador, tried to separate them with its nose. Talk about bad timing. James pulled away from Lauren.

An elderly couple hurried up and pulled the dog's leash tighter. The old man, wearing a Yankees cap and Mets T–shirt, smiled. "I'm sorry. Isla always gets jealous when she sees me kissing the missus like that."

"Stop telling tales." The white–haired woman with rosy cheeks swatted his thin arm. "I told you to keep that dog of yours on a shorter leash."

"Fifty years of marriage and she's still telling me what to do." The man laughed. "We'll be on our way. You two get back to what you were doing."

He stared at Lauren. Wide–eyed, flushed cheeks and swollen lips, she looked utterly and thoroughly kissed.

Lauren's heart was racing away and she just blurted it out.

"Can we try for a baby?"

James looked shocked and took a step back. Lauren felt even more nervous now.

"Err, never really thought about it. What about your job?"

Lauren, by now, had become a bit more composed and felt a bit upset with the question. She now felt a little unsure.

James saw the sadness in her eyes and quickly retorted.

"Sure, why not? You just caught me a little off guard. I knew we would always have children one day, just was not quite expecting it yet. What do you want to do next?"

Lauren burst out laughing. "Well James, do you want me to tell you or demonstrate what you need to do?"

James realised what he had said and blushed slightly, but the unintentional comment had made things better.

"We can start on Operation Baby as soon as we get home then," said James.

Lauren laughed and retorted, "Will you give a briefing beforehand then?"

CHAPTER NINE – PROBATIONER PROBLEMS

Back at work after four days off, Lauren had plenty of paperwork to get through. Being a sergeant was harder than being a PC. She had to produce reports as well as professional development reviews on her team. She had a review to do on a PC Tom Atkin, mainly through necessity. He only had six months' service, but was proving to be a bit of a liability and the rest of the shift was concerned that he was not up to the job. Tom seemed in a different world to everyone else. Ask him what he had just seen and he could not remember. He had passed all the police recruitment assessments and done well at training school. However, out on the street, his practical policing was awful and he just fell apart the moment he stepped out of the station.

Two incidents she really needed to discuss with Tom included one that only happened last week. Tom was on foot patrol with a PCSO and they were walking through the park. The PCSO thought she saw one of them smoking cannabis so stopped both the males. Tom did a search and found nothing, and then the male picked up the butt he had been smoking that still contained cannabis. He asked Tom what he should do with it and Tom replied, "Just throw it in the bushes."

Even though it was only a butt, the male was still in possession of cannabis, and throwing it into some bushes meant the evidence had be thrown away in an unsafe manner.

The PCSO had been concerned and had reported it to her sergeant, who had spoken to Lauren. The other incident was with a pizza delivery guy Tom had seen speeding. He had followed the car back to the car park across the road from the pizza takeaway and, instead of just speaking to him, had lost his rag and started shouting and really laying into the guy. The pizza guy had complained about Tom and how he had been treated by him.

It was not the sort of review Lauren was looking forward to undertaking. She felt it was going to be a case where he either pulled his socks up or would be asked to resign. The strange part was that he had been a decent special constable for a year previously. However, his lack of skills seemed to point to a lack of real experience. Lauren wondered what he had done for a year as a special and why anyone did not pick up any problems with him.

The other, more important job was to inform her inspector and HR that she was pregnant. She knew that the moment she told them, she would be put on light duties. Light duties meant pretty much flying a desk and being non-operational.

Lauren enjoyed being out on the street and, even as a sergeant, liked to get hands-on and stuck in when she could.

She had only told James the week before that she was pregnant after feeling sick and taking a pregnancy test. She had been to the doctors and he confirmed she was expecting. The next milestone in a few weeks would be the first scan to check that everything was OK.

Briefing was quite a relaxed affair today, Amy had brought in some doughnuts for everyone and Lauren announced she was pregnant to the shift, which prompted applause from everyone along with congratulations, followed by questions on when the baby was due and who the father was!

With briefing finished, she decided to get on with Tom's review. It was not actually as bad as she thought. Tom actually said in the review before she had covered any issues with him that he was thinking of quitting, as being a police officer was not really what he wanted to do. With this, Lauren decided to hold off with the review points and told Tom to have a good think about it over this set of shifts before making a firm decision about what he wanted to when he came back. If he decided to stay, Lauren would then talk about the issues and how he could be supported to improve.

By the time she had finished the review, the whole station knew that Lauren was pregnant and the congratulations came flooding in. Lauren was sure by the end of the day the whole force would know.

At 9am, Lauren's inspector strolled in and Lauren asked to have a word with him. She got on well with Inspector Langton; he was in his late forties and an easy-going person. In addition, he was someone who would stand by his officers. Before she had the chance to tell him, he already knew Lauren was pregnant. Lauren still wanted to have a chat with the inspector about Tom and the various issues. He agreed and understood Lauren's actions, although he said all probationers make mistakes and proceeded to tell Lauren of the ones he had made as a young PC.

As a probationer PC, he was coming to the end of a night shift at the police station when an officer summoned him to the front desk.

"PC Langton, you'd best have a listen to what this chap wants to say," he was told, and he was directed towards a well-known local man of Polish descent who was sitting in the reception area, looking decidedly fidgety. At the time, this male, who was well-built was known to be homeless and of no fixed abode, and was around town at all times of the day and night. He was the type who seemed harmless enough but you would not want to meet him in a dark alley.

Intrigued, PC Langton went over and sat next to the man.

"You have something you want to tell me?" he asked.

Looking increasingly shifty, the man replied in a strong Polish accent, "Yes... I need to tell... I have just killed little girl."

Langton's jaw dropped and, uncertain he had heard correctly, he asked, "You've done what?"

"I have just killed little girl. I feel bad."

Langton's mind raced. What do I do next? He ushered the man into a side room and told him to sit and wait, instructing another PC to watch the man closely. He then phoned the DI at home, waking him to give him the news that a man had just walked into the station confessing to a murder.

"Are you sure about this, PC Langton?" growled the DI down the phone.

"Yes sir... he's here now and has just told me he's killed a child."

"Keep him there. I will be down shortly and I'll bring the cavalry with me," barked the DI, "and get more information from him if you can."

Langton went back to the man and started an informal chat.

Langton started, "When did this happen?"

"This morning, just before I come here."

"Where did you do it?"

"Behind church."

"And this girl you killed... what did she look like?"

At this, the man seemed puzzled.

"She looks like all the others," he replied.

Langton then thought, is this guy a serial killer?

"Why did you kill her?"

"She hurt, she could not fly properly so I kill her, I stamp on head and she die."

"Fly??? Hang on a second, what is this man on about?" he thought.

"Err... you said you killed a little GIRL?" said Langton

The man looked for a minute, and then burst into a loud laugh, much to Langton's bemusement and annoyance.

"GULL, I kill GULL," he said in his thick accent. "Little gull, you know, flap flap." He flapped his arms and did his best to impersonate the screech of a seagull.

Inspector Langton got some stick about that one for years, and received bird feathers and real eggs in his docket randomly afterwards. He is still known as the gullible inspector!

Chapter Ten – Left Holding the Baby

Three days after Lauren's due date, the baby was still in no hurry to meet its parents. Up until now, Lauren's pregnancy had been straightforward, but when she went to the clinic the doctor was a little concerned about the size of the baby.

Lauren was booked in for an ultrasound. The news was that the baby's head was very low and that it roughly weighed a manageable 7lbs 8oz - so far so good. Lauren checked in again at the clinic, where the midwife did a quick internal examination.

"Actually, you're three centimetres dilated already," the midwife said with a smile.

That was the first in a series of shocks that James was to experience over the next four days.

Although James was desperately looking forward to meeting his son or daughter, he had found it hard to grasp the concept that the lump in his wife's stomach was actually going to become his baby. Through all the sickness, backache, swollen ankles and relentless kicking, Lauren had already formed a very close bond with her "bump."

"Go home and if nothing happens overnight, come in tomorrow morning at nine," said the midwife. So back they went. Everything seemed to be going fine at home, and despite the fact Lauren was three centimetres dilated, she wasn't in any pain, so she wondered quite seriously whether she was going to be one of the lucky few who experienced a 'silent labour'.

A couple of hours later she had some bleeding, and, staying close to the instructions in all the books, James rang the hospital to say they were on their way. They wanted to keep Lauren in overnight. James spent a restless night at home without his wife for the first time, waiting for a phone call to say Lauren had gone into labour. However, it did not come, which meant James made his way back to hospital the next morning. Lauren was fully expecting to be induced.

For some unknown reason, countless other couples seemed to have the same due date as James and Lauren, and it was like national birth weekend at the hospital. They had to wait early on Sunday morning for a space on the maternity ward. James found it a nerve-wracking few days and was thoroughly exhausted with worry.

Nearly three days later than expected, Lauren's waters finally broke while she was waiting to be induced. James had never seen anything like it; he could not believe that Lauren had managed to keep what appeared to be two or three large bucketfuls of liquid inside her for so long.

As time went on, Lauren started having mild contractions, combined with a return of the back pain she'd had earlier in the pregnancy. Gradually, the contractions intensified and, with the back pain causing her to be sick, Lauren decided she needed an epidural. James had felt like a spare part during most of Lauren's nine-month pregnancy, but right now he felt truly useless and the feeling got worse.

Lauren found it easier to push while on her side, and she was doing really well. James spoke to a colleague on his shift who had been quite embarrassed at managing to pass out during his daughter's birth. This same colleague had been to shootings, stabbings and fatal RTCs, only to succumb to the birth of his own daughter. This had made James a bit nervous about watching the delivery itself. However, once the midwife said she could see the top of the head, he could not resist.

Despite James' feelings of inadequacy, the midwife encouraged him to be as involved as possible. Not only did James try to offer words of support from time to time, even whilst Lauren was swearing like a trooper, he was given the task of preparing the new born baby's clothes and putting bedding in the cot. He was also asked if he wanted to cut the cord once the baby had been delivered.

Lauren needed an episiotomy to make things easier, and after less than an hour's pushing, at 1.58pm, baby Luke shot out into the delivery room - a whopping 8lbs 15oz. To James' immense relief, baby Luke started to cry almost immediately. James had just watched his son emerge into the world; it was a fantastic, frightening, exhilarating experience which he felt privileged to have witnessed. Both James and Lauren felt elated and tears came to both of their eyes, even though James fought hard to hold his back

Once Luke had been born, James' automatic reaction was to relax, but it was not over yet. As the placenta was delivered, Lauren lost quite a lot of blood. Her blood pressure plummeted and before James knew it, he was in the middle of a scene from ER, and literally left holding the baby while four or five staff gave the necessary aid to Lauren.

Lauren needed four units of blood and was not allowed back onto the ward until she had had an operation for a retained placenta, as not all of the placenta had come out during childbirth.

With Lauren being told to rest, James was given basic lessons in bathing, dressing, and nappy changing; the upside was at least he had the opportunity to get to know his baby son and to be of some practical use.

A day or so later, after Lauren had recovered, James was finally able to realise that he had become a father. An amazing feeling, thought James, even though the birth had been far from easy.

Chapter Eleven – Life Changing

With baby Luke and Lauren back home, James felt much happier, and it took a few days to get into the routine of feeds every four to five hours. Both James' and Lauren's mums had offered to pop round and help when James had finished his paternity leave in just over a week's time. James, in some ways, was looking forward to going back to work as it seemed the easy option compared to dealing with a baby that just ate, slept and filled his nappy.

Baby Luke really had changed their lives within a matter of days. Their whole life revolved around the baby's needs. Even Maisy would take guard duty outside the nursery door and was very protective of Luke, patrolling outside the door like a soldier on sentry duty. The worst part of having a newborn baby was the sleep deprivation and only having a few hours' sleep before being woken up for the next feed. Lauren initially just breast-fed, but found it was too difficult day and night. She switched to bottles in the night and breast during the day, much to the midwife's displeasure.

James got into a bit of a routine; he would take Maisy out for a walk, along with Luke in his pram. More often than not, women with children or old women would stop to coo at Luke. Luke seemed to already know exactly when to smile to get the most attention.

Lauren enjoyed having James about the house, and would miss the adult conversation when he went back to work. James being on nights would be the worst; when she was sleeping, he would be at work, and then the reverse during the day.

After two weeks' paternity leave, it was back to work and straight onto a night shift. John was glad to have James back. For two people with such different backgrounds, one who had been to university and gained a degree, the other a few GCSEs and the University of Life, James and John got on and worked well together. James was the better communicator and John the tactician with good situational awareness.

So far, the shift had not been too busy. They had caught a drunk driver within the first hour of duty, acted as back-up to a fight, and carried out an area search after a robbery.

At 2am, James and John were called to a job in the city centre following reports of a stabbing where the offender had made off. A 35-year-old man was in a critical condition after being stabbed. The man had been stabbed several times on Bow Lane, and the offender had been seen running to the Ruby Tuesday bar. The stabbing had occurred following an altercation in the street between two groups of males. A silver-coloured saloon car was seen in the area shortly afterwards and thought to be connected. CCTV had caught the male on camera and witnesses had described the offender as a white man, about 5ft 6in tall, bald and with a thin goatee-style beard.

Paramedics were already on scene treating the male, along with local police. James and John had been sent due to the violent nature of the offence and because the offender was still at large. John decided the best course of action was to circle the city centre looking for either the male or the silver car.

They did one loop and found nothing. Then, as they went round again, James spotted a silver saloon at the traffic lights that could well match the description. John radioed it through to alert other units, just in case. They sat behind the car and waited for it to pull off, before putting on the blue lights just before the entrance to a car park. The car signalled to pull over and went into the car park, before coming to a stop.

James stepped out and as soon as he had taken two steps, the car sped up the ramp into the multi-storey car park. James jumped back in the car and they took off after it. The guy driving it was using his handbrake on the corners. John, with all his skill, was struggling to keep up in the Land Rover Discovery.

The car was now about a floor ahead and nearing the top of the car park. On reaching the final level, James and John could see the car abandoned with the passenger and driver's doors open, but there was no sign of anybody. James got another unit to stay at the ground floor and requested a police dog to try to follow the scent. Within minutes, three police cars were covering all the exits out of the car park.

John went over to check the car out whilst James used the vantage point to see if anyone came out. After about 5 minutes, a male appeared out of one exit, although he did not match the description. The cops below detained him to find out who he was. Meanwhile, John checked the silver saloon's registration, and it turned out to be an Audi A4 that belonged to a Daljit Rai. The guy below said his name was Raj Mahwah and he had no ID on him to prove who he was. John's gut told him he was most probably this Daljit Rai and, on opening the glove box, the smell of sweaty feet hit him. In the glove box, he found several bags containing crack cocaine. No surprise that he wanted to hide his identity.

After a fingerprint check on the Lantern, Raj Mahwah did turn out to be Daljit Rai, a known drug dealer who was wanted for drugs charges. Within five minutes of arresting him, the male they wanted in connection with the stabbing was found, and in his pocket was a wrap of crack cocaine. The passenger in the car had somehow managed to slip away into the night. The car and the drugs needed to be seized and Daljit was carted off to custody. James recovered the keys and had the pleasure of driving the car, which reeked of crack cocaine and freshly smoked cannabis, back to base for a forensic examination.

Walking back through his front door at 7:30am, James was greeted by a rather white and worried-looking Lauren. She was still suffering some blood loss after the birth of Luke, but last night a rather larger piece of placenta had come out and her loss of blood had increased. She had been in pain over the past two weeks, and the midwife thought it was just her insides settling down after childbirth.

James got her to lie down on the sofa; baby Luke was fast asleep, unaware of his poorly mother. With Lauren looking as if she was going into shock, James rang 999 for an ambulance. As he spoke, he could feel himself shaking and losing the composure he would normally have on duty. It was so different when it was a loved one who was suffering. He gave the control room operator all the details and someone was dispatched straight away. Within five minutes, a fast response car had arrived and knocked on the door, whilst James got on the phone to his parents asking if they could come and babysit.

The paramedic took Lauren's blood pressure and heart rate, and put a cannula into her arm just in case a drip was needed. He then radioed through for an ambulance to take her to hospital. Due to the type and nature of the bleed, a female crew had been called.

James could feel himself welling up inside as the concern and worry took hold. As the ambulance arrived, so did James' parents, who were a very comforting sight. His mum came in and checked on the baby, at the same time being supportive to James.

It was only a short drive to hospital in the ambulance, where Lauren was wheeled into A&E waiting to be seen. A line of beds with people on them lined the corridors. A young doctor came up to Lauren and asked if he could take a blood sample. The young doctor turned out to be a student. His trembling hands made it hard for him to get the needle in properly. After four tries and a few winces from Lauren, he managed to take two samples.

After an hour's wait, a doctor came to see Lauren, checked her abdomen, asked a few questions and made the decision to send her back to the maternity ward. She did have some form of infection that could be due to a retained placenta, but would know more lately after various checks and tests.

It looked like James would not get much sleep today; he did quite a bit of hanging around with Lauren in hospital. However, he would rather be at Lauren's side than anywhere else, even if that meant not having any sleep. He would also need to inform his sergeant that he would not make the second night shift, which was also, thankfully, his last before he had four days off.

Lauren got her own room this time, instead of the ward she had been on after the birth of Luke.

She was checked over and it was confirmed that she had a retained placenta, although it seemed most of it had come out. She was scheduled to have any remaining placenta removed and was placed on antibiotics to quell the infection. She would be in overnight and it was hoped that they would be able to discharge her the next day.

By late afternoon, James was really starting to flag and feeling very tired after being awake for 20 hours. He rang his dad to come and collect him, so at least he could get a few hours' kip before his parents went home and Luke needed a feed.

Luke only required one feed in the night, although James did find it a bit scary being left with a newborn baby to look after by himself and felt very inadequate.

The next day, James took Luke with him to go and collect Lauren from hospital. Lauren was so glad to see Luke; she had missed him. She had found it very difficult to sleep, not having either James or Luke with her, although the peace and quiet had been nice, as had getting an undisturbed night's sleep.

CHAPTER TWELVE - MURDER

Baby Luke was growing fast; he was already too big for his Moses basket and needed to be in a cot. Lauren had changed from a career cop to a very devoting mother, and having a baby had changed the way she viewed life.

James felt content with his life, although he did find that working shifts meant he did not get as much family time as he had hoped he would.

Back on days, James and John had been called to reports of a male who was high on drink and drugs, strolling down the street clutching a 13-inch knife he had just used.

The male was a known drug addict called Darren Stokes. He had just stabbed his girlfriend, a mother-of-one, multiple times in the chest in a frenzied attack at their home. He then threw a duvet over the 22-year-old as she lay dying, and walked out holding the murder weapon, saying he had left her for dead according to witnesses on the street

He had been due in court the day before to hear charges of assault and drugs possession. However, he had failed to appear and a warrant for his arrest had only just been circulated.

With a direction of travel and with CCTV following him, James and John raced to the area. Initially Darren could not be found, but one witness suggested trying his brother's house.

James and John got out with tasers drawn, just in case, and banged loudly on the front door. Darren's brother came to the door and James noticed blood on one of his hands. John pushed the brother aside and went in to search the house.

They found Darren upstairs, hiding under a duvet, covered in blood.

Darren kept saying, "She's dead, she's dead, no-one is going to have her now."

Local police had also found the discarded knife in a front garden not too far from Darren's home address. Within 45 minutes of the call, they had managed to apprehend the offender and recover the murder weapon; a good result in tragic circumstances.

Once they had finished booking in Stokes, James and John got their next call to a suicide attempt. The caller had allegedly taken an intentional overdose of prescription medication in an attempt to harm himself. Despite the fact that he called the police, the subject told control that he did not want the police to respond. He added that he had barricaded himself in his bedroom.

Whilst travelling to the call, control said the subject sounded like he may be losing consciousness. Control maintained contact with the caller for as long as possible. They advised that the caller had been known to carry a weapon. Upon arrival, two other officers met with James and John a few houses from the male's residence to formulate a plan. John got control to call the male again, but they received no answer. As they began walking toward the house, they saw a vehicle parked in the driveway and a young couple with a baby entering the house. Fearing that the couple had unknowingly placed themselves and their baby in danger, they decided to enter the house to evacuate them and attempt to contact the suicidal male.

Once inside the house, they located the couple and their baby and directed them outside. The couple explained to James that they had rented a room inside the residence, as had the suicidal male. They mentioned that there were likely other people in the residence, but were unable to confirm whether anyone else was home because all the flat doors were locked. The couple pointed out the suicidal male's window and they all made their way upstairs to contact him.

John tried to talk to the male, "Hey mate, it is the police. We just want to talk to you. Open the door, we need to make sure you're alright."

The man did not reply and just started to grunt.

John tried negotiating with the male to open the door for several minutes; he became more hostile, as he swore, yelled and became more hysterical. John kicked in the flimsy bedroom door with an enforcer. Upon impact, the door was literally ripped in half, and the ram penetrated a wooden dresser that the male had propped against the door. As soon as the door was open, James backed away from the doorway and drew his taser, as the other officers pointed their Gloks at the subject.

The man was standing in an aggressive stance near the front door, holding a large fixed-blade knife in his left hand. James could not see his right hand because he kept it behind the dresser that had been used to barricade the door.

James pointed his taser at the subject as John and the other two Armed Response officers provided lethal force cover with their handguns, ready to engage if needed.

James said, "Drop the knife or I will use the taser. Drop the knife."

When the male disobeyed all verbal commands to drop the knife, James fired the taser, causing both probes to imbed in the man's chest area. The man fell to the floor immobile, and John rushed in to handcuff him without further incident.

Once back in custody, the suicidal male thanked James for having used his taser to subdue him. He mentioned that had it not been for the police, he would have killed himself that day. He was assessed before being given a psychiatric assessment and admitted to hospital for mental health problems.

John never really spoke about his family or anyone else. He seemed to pretty much talk about the police, the army and fit women, in that order. James had broached the subject once before and John had changed it, being rather coy. James tried again and John brushed it off, but not before mentioning the name Claire. Was this his girlfriend or wife?

John decided to tell one of his jokes as a deflection.

"A burglar broke into a house one night. He shone his flashlight around, looking for valuables, and when he picked up a CD player to place in his sack, a strange disembodied voice echoed from the dark saying, "Jesus is watching YOU."

He nearly jumped out of his skin, clicked his flashlight out and froze. When he heard nothing more after a bit, he shook his head, promised himself a holiday after the next big haul, then clicked the light back on and began searching for more valuables. Just as he pulled the stereo out so he could disconnect the wires, clear as a bell, he heard "Jesus is watching you."

Freaked out, he shone his light around frantically, looking for the source of the voice. Finally, in the corner of the room, his flashlight beam came to rest on a parrot.

"Did you say that?" he hissed at the parrot.

"Yep," the parrot confessed, and then squawked, "I'm trying to warn you."

The burglar relaxed. "Warn me, huh? Who are you?"

"Moses," replied the parrot. "Moses?" the burglar laughed. "What kind of stupid person would name a parrot Moses?"

"Probably the same kind of person who would name a Rottweiler Jesus."

Chapter Thirteen – Shopping Revelations

The hustle and bustle of a Saturday morning shopping was too much for James; he had always avoided shopping in the city centre on a Saturday like the plague. With the sales on, Lauren had decreed they needed to go shopping as Luke needed some new clothes. James thought it was just an excuse to go shopping, but kept quiet rather than cause an unnecessary argument.

After about the third shop, James was already fed up and desperate to go home. He felt like a bored teenager slowly getting stroppy as he craved something more interesting to do. Lauren was in her element looking for the perfect outfits to put Luke in and cooing at all the cute clothes. She announced to James that she wanted a girl next, as the choice of clothes for girls was so much wider than for boys.

James decided to say nothing and gazed around the store, just in case there was something more interesting to go and look at. Then out of the corner of his eye, he noticed a well-built man with cropped brown hair. The male, who was with a woman, looked like John. Sure enough, as he got closer, it was John.

John seemed a bit startled to see James and kept his head low as he approached.

"Hiya mate," said James

"Alright mate," John replied

Lauren then turned around and was both startled and surprised at the same time. John was with her sister Helena.

Helena stood there, immaculately dressed in this season's must-have dress with her long brunette hair straightened and wearing full make-up. Dressed up like that, Lauren knew this must be serious.

"Sis, you never told me you were seeing anyone. Never mind that you were dating John, who works with James!"

"Yeah I know, we have not been together that long. I wanted to keep it quiet for the moment, with John and James working together."

James just said, "You're the man John," without really thinking, and got a stern look from Lauren.

"You have taken me by surprise Helena, but I am really happy for you. When did you meet?"

"I was actually on a date with Paul when I first met John. Paul had the idea to go to the seaside. Though I liked him enough, I did think he was off his rocker to have dragged me to the seaside for the afternoon.

We went for a walk along the front and then down to the sea wall made up of large rocks. As the rocks came into view, the wind blew a little chillier and I held tighter to Paul's hand, mostly for warmth. I looked up and standing across from me, on one of the larger rocks, was a man. I could not see his face; his back was to me as he was scanning the horizon. I was intrigued as to what he was doing and, to be honest, he looked quite fit.

I sat on one of the nearby rocks looking out to sea and a petite woman came over and lit a cigarette. Clearly pleased to have found another person to talk to, she began telling me her life story. Her doctor husband had slept with his nurse and they were now in the process of a divorce. Her life was a mess, and she was very depressed. Her brother had brought her here today to get her to forget about her

216

woes and enjoy the sea air. Then she asked if I was there with anyone. I pointed to my date, and realised he was standing and chatting with the man I had been ogling on the rocks.

"Oh, he's talking to my brother," said the woman.

The two men were walking back toward us and for the first time, I saw the face of the other man. There was something about him that I was instantly attracted to.

The four of us spent the rest of the day together. The entire time, my thoughts kept swapping partners. I decided somewhere along the way that my date and the distraught woman would make much better companions and that I needed to get to know the man she was with better. At the end of the day, we all exchanged phone numbers and went our separate ways.

I still could not get the man out of my head and realised that Paul was not right for me; it was not a match. There simply was not enough in common. The next day, I received a call. It was John. He asked how serious I was with the man I had been with a few days before. I told him we had actually broken up. There was a deep sigh on the other end of the phone and the words: "Then you're free for dinner?"

I replied yes in an instant and we went out. I still had no idea what John did for a living or that he worked with James. On the third date I started talking about Lauren and that she was a police officer, and the penny dropped with John."

John had gone a little sheepish, almost as if he had betrayed a friend, but James was not bothered at all. He knew and trusted John, even if he was a grumpy old sod at times. However, James could imagine some awkward conversations with Lauren when she tried to get James to collect all the gossip on what was going on with John and her sister.

Chapter Fourteen - Spiderman

Back on days with John after four days off, James decided he would leave it up to John if he wanted to talk about Helena or not. There did seem to be some tension, so John told another one of his "war stories" as if to break the tension. This time it was about when he was a recruit out on exercise.

John had done his basic soldier training at Catterick in Yorkshire, which is not known for its weather. It was April and still bitterly cold, so cold that it had been snowing. They had been issued with winter rations that were approaching their use-by date, which was fine except that they consisted of boiled rice and rehydrated food that needed plenty of water heat to cook. The normal boil-in-the-bag stuff could be eaten hot or cold.

John had been told to go out and put out trip flares. These were just a flare with a long wire attached that would go off if walked through, alerting everyone to a potential attack.

This had taken so long that it was getting dark, so no sooner had John started cooking his food than he was ordered to stop and put the fire out. The food was still raw and he attempted to eat semi-raw rice and peas, along with a cup of tepid tea.

The night temperature really dropped and, even in his sleeping bag, John was shivering like a leaf. He knew he was on the verge of hypothermia. However, if he gave up he would be back squadded and he would have to report the previous three weeks. John just had to ride the night out, one of the longest he had ever known. The next day, warm sunshine woke John up, although he still felt rather ill as he emerged from his basha made from bungee cords and a waterproof sheet.

The next night was not much better; they all had to dig trenches and sleep in them. Only these just filled with water and mud, and John spent his second night sleeping in muddy water. The sleeping bags had a Gortex outer that they could be put in, so at least you stayed semi-dry.

John then said, "If that is what a water bed is like, you can forget me ever getting one."

James and John got their first call of the shift; a sex offender had broken his bail conditions for the sixth time and was wanted for "breach of bail." A PCSO had spotted him in the city centre and tried to follow him, but had lost him in the city centre crowds. They had a direction of travel, and everyone got told to make their way to the area. The police helicopter was scrambled to aid in the search. As James and John got into the area where the male had last been sighted, he was reported to have been seen by another unit heading towards the park. James and John went to one entrance whilst the helicopter buzzed overhead, trying to locate the male.

It seemed he had gone to ground, so the helicopter decided to move away and come back after he had appeared, as the noise of the helicopter meant he was probably keeping his head down until it had gone.

Sure enough, the moment the police helicopter had moved away, the man appeared and was reported to be running towards James and John. James ran towards him but just before they met, the man had jumped onto a wall and then onto the roof of a pub.

John could see the man on the roof and shouted up, "It's all over mate, best to get yourself down."

James said, "Come on; do us all a favour, no point staying up there all day."

With this, the man turned and ran off in a different direction, jumping across another roof and onto some garages before jumping down and over a fence. The helicopter was overhead, following his every move and directing officers to where he was.

"Bloomin' hell, he is like Spiderman," John said.

James and John were still in hot pursuit but could not keep up with the man. He ran down another alley and was spotted by local police, who took up the chase and finally managed to catch him. By the time John and James had got to them, the male was already in handcuffs and being picked up off the floor before being carted off to custody.

John finally got round to talking about Helena.

"She is amazing you know James, in all senses of the word." John gave a big grin.

"You certainly kept it quiet."

"I know Helena did not want to say anything until we had been going out a while, but you and Lauren sprang us! I have no idea why she wanted to keep it quiet. I got the impression she thought Lauren and her parents would disapprove or something?"

"Yeah, you could be right," said James.

James then proceeded to ask questions about John's previous romantic history. John was still a bit cagey about his past, but did drop that he had been married in the army for a short time. However, whilst he was away on a six-month tour, his wife had an affair with another soldier. John was devastated and vowed to keep away from women for as long as possible, seeing them as "snakes with tits." Other than a short relationship with a woman with three kids a few years back, John had shied away from relationships, preferring to focus on his job and the odd "fuck buddy."

Helena had come along like a breath of fresh air and put some fun back into his life. She could get a bit too silly at times for "serious John," but at the same time, James could tell he had really fallen for her.

Chapter Fifteen – Fully Armed

Today was an early 5am start for James; the whole Armed Response team was to be in briefing by 6am. Today they were going to carry out a raid on a suspected drugs and arms dealer. Armed Response was to go in first, before CID officers and local police. Capturing the targets and seizing evidence was the main priority. Key members of the cartel had been put under surveillance for the past six years, and even had their phones and homes tapped and bugged. The cartel had been an issue for the past seven years and it had proved hard to get to the ones at the top. The last head of the cartel had disappeared mysteriously four years ago, and then Laurence Chapman had replaced them. The same Laurence Chapman that Lauren had been at school with. Various raids had harmed the supply, but as always, new dealers would step in and carry on the supply of drugs.

According to intelligence, a shipment of both drugs and guns had arrived at the warehouse. The newish warehouse had only just been rented. It was situated at the back of a large industrial estate, almost hidden away. When a large shipment came in, Laurence would always visit to check the order, but would vary the time and period after the shipment had arrived to avoid a raid taking place and getting arrested. A raid six months ago at a takeaway used as a front for drugs distribution had missed Laurence by a few minutes. The belief was that Laurence had been tipped off to the raid from someone within the police. Laurence had several cops on his payroll to feed him intelligence. Even though a couple of officers had been arrested and subsequently sacked from the service a few years ago, information was still being passed. The cartel was linked to the shooting of Kevin Doughty five years ago over a £20,000 debt. They had the person who had shot Kevin. However, he had not revealed anything other than that he was acting alone. If he had revealed anything, he would have most probably been killed.

Laurence started out as door staff working in several nightclubs, and that was where he started dealing. He learnt about the drugs trade by controlling access of dealers into and out of the club initially, before getting them to supply him directly, then later he began to traffic drugs. To cover up his drugs business, he set up a legitimate security company that supplied door staff to the various pubs and clubs. Other firms were threatened with violence to stay away. This meant Laurence had the monopoly on door staff in nearly all the clubs and bars in the city centre. With that, he was better able to control the supply of drugs and slowly set up his own supply chain. He had made several links for trafficking heroin in the Netherlands and had several cannabis farms both within the city and nationally. Laurence was a very violent man and ruled his cartel with fear and intimidation. To anyone outside the cartel though, Laurence came across as a kind and thoughtful person who regularly gave money to charity.

The cartel would set up a new grow or stash, and move the cannabis farms around regularly to reduce the risk of the stash or grow being found. The use of rented houses and small warehouses made them very easy to move, especially if Laurence got word of a raid.

The problem had been in getting witnesses, as these had all been either threatened with violence or killed. Any killings were often carried out outside of the city to lessen the trail back to the cartel. Laurence had two hit men on his payroll. One hit man was due in court for murder, and the other one was still at large due to a lack of evidence.

The briefing James was sitting in was very thorough, with every exit and entry point covered as well as what the various commands were to execute the raid. Due to the very high likelihood of weapons being present, everyone would go in with their MP5s and full tactical equipment, including helmets.

James was very grateful to be with John. He soaked up all the orders and James could see him formulating a plan in his own mind. John's previous experience would prove invaluable, even though lethal force was a last resort and a hard arrest was much preferred.

With briefing complete, it was time for everyone to pile into the vans; they would probably have to spend many hours in a hold-up position until Laurence and his associates turned up. Laurence would also have his bodyguards with him, who would most certainly be carrying firearms.

The surveillance team had positioned themselves in a warehouse a short distance from Laurence's own. They would be the ones who would communicate when Laurence was on site.

After three hours in the police van, the team were growing restless and a little bit bored, when finally the radio crackled into life. Laurence and his bodyguards were reported to be entering the warehouse. The two vans containing Armed Response moved up to their strike position, just around the corner from the warehouse. James, John, Alan and Ady were given an entry point via a fire exit. One team would enter through the main entrance and another through the rear.

All the teams moved in, knowing the minute they were in the perimeter they would be spotted. The idea was to swoop in fast and make the hard arrests before any weapons could be drawn.

John took the lead and rushed towards the fire exit. By now, the nerves James had felt in the build-up to the raid had passed. His training simply kicked in. John used the enforcer to bash the fire exit door open and they burst through, shouting,

"ARMED POLICE OFFICERS. Put your weapons down and hands up."

Even though they had moved in fast, Laurence and his cartel had been alerted. The minute the police entered, three shots could be heard. The team coming through the front of the warehouse were fired upon and they quickly arrested the spotter at the front, followed by another male in quick succession. Both were carrying a handgun and a knife.

The third team was moving in from the rear, which had the effect of the other targets moving upstairs exactly where John, James, Alan, and Ady were moving through. As John turned the corner to move out of an office, one of the bodyguards discharged another shot. This hit John squarely in the shoulder, pushing him back on top of James. Alan returned with a shot, but missed.

Ady radioed in to say John had been hit, putting the paramedics who were on standby ready to move in and treat him when they were given the all clear.

James stayed with John as Ady and Alan moved forward. The team downstairs moved quickly upstairs as back-up.

The upstairs area was made up of walkways that led to a storeroom and several offices. On the side of one office was the fire exit that James and the others had come through. With Alan and Ady pushing forward, John insisted that James covered them. James got John to rest up against a wall in one of the offices.

James moved forward to catch up with Alan and Ady when, out of the corner of his eye, he saw a glint of metal. He spun round on his feet to one of the bodyguards standing with a gun pointed squarely at him. Without time to react, James fired and hit the bodyguard in the chest, sending him backwards before he fell and hit the floor with a loud thud.

Meanwhile, Alan and Ady had caught up with Laurence and another bodyguard as they tried to double back through the offices and escape through the fire exit.

With this done, the other two teams shouted "Clear," and it was safe for local officers, CID and paramedics to enter.

James, on exiting the building, immediately had his weapon and ammunition seized and bagged as evidence. He was also debriefed before leaving the scene.

The man he shot had died whilst the paramedics tried to work on him. John was OK, other than having his pride wounded and sustaining a non-life threatening gunshot wound.

He kept saying, "I have never been shot, I have never been shot before. All that time in the army and not a scratch, and I get bloomin' shot in the police."

As soon as James got back to the station, he went into the toilet and threw up. The mixture of shock and adrenalin had taken its toll. James was only just starting to realise that he had killed someone and his mind kept replaying the moment he had shot the bodyguard. Everything was in slow motion as he worked through what had happened. James could almost see the bullet leaving his gun. Could he have shot him and not killed him? If he had not shot him, would he now be wounded or dead? The feeling of guilt welled up inside James, and he felt close to tears.

Everyone was patting him on the back and saying he did a good job in difficult circumstances. The fatal shooting would have to be investigated by the Independent Police Complaints Committee.

James was given a few days' mandatory leave before he could return; whilst the initial investigation took place, he was placed on restricted duty.

The shooting and capture of Laurence Chapman had caused a stir in the media and an outcry from the community of the dead bodyguard, Pete Rathbone. Pete had worked on the doors of clubs for years and slowly worked his way up the ladder before getting 'the top job' of Laurence Chapman's bodyguard. James still felt extremely guilty about killing someone; he struggled to come to terms with what had happened. Lauren had to put up with a very moody and at times angry James, the complete opposite to his usual cheery self. Lauren was concerned about him and said he really should see the force counsellor as he was probably suffering PTSD.

Lauren read up on PTSD; she had heard about it and sadly dealt with soldiers who had committed violent acts or suicide after coming back from Afghanistan.

"Post-traumatic stress disorder is a type of anxiety disorder. It can occur after you've seen or experienced a traumatic event that involved the threat of injury or death."

James denied he was suffering PTSD, and just said that he was tired and felt guilty about shooting someone.

James did agree to see a counsellor as he could see the worry and anxiety on Lauren's face.

John phoned James to read out an email that had been sent to the whole Armed Response team by the IPCC. John was also on restricted duties whilst his shoulder fully recovered. It was a clean shot with the bullet passing straight through with minimal damage. He had been lucky, as he always seemed to be.

"The Independent Police Complaints Commission has completed an assessment into a fatal shooting of Pete Rathbone last week and has determined there is no requirement for an IPCC investigation.

An Armed Response operation attempted to arrest several armed and dangerous suspects and came under fire.

We have conducted a thorough and independent assessment of all the available information, including viewing video footage and witness statements. On the basis of the information we have seen, the IPCC is confident all officers involved observed all necessary policies and procedures and the use of lethal force was used to protect life.

As a result, the IPCC is content for the investigation into this incident to be carried out by the force."

There was a silent pause, and then John said,

"Mate, it's all over. You can get back on operational duty. You probably saved not only your life but mine as well. It was a case of kill or be killed. If it makes you feel any better, I felt just the same when I had to kill my first person; it haunted me for weeks until I realised it was him or me."

James just replied, "Yeah."

He was still trying to take it all in and he was unsure whether he wanted to stay in Armed Response. He had not joined the police to kill anyone, and on joining Armed Response, had never expected he would ever be in the position to have killed someone. Looking across at Luke, he also felt guilty that he had put himself in danger and that his son could have grown up without a father.

James made the decision to leave Armed Response to become a Beat Manager, looking after a local area and working closely with the community. The hours were slightly better, with night shifts usually being until midnight or 1am. James really enjoyed being part of the local community and it meant he was able to see more of his son and Lauren.

It took James six months to get over the shooting, and he still had the odd nightmare. Counselling helped, as did the loving support from Lauren.

Six months after the shooting, John drove past in the ARV with blue lights flashing, wound his window down, and shouted,

"I am getting married to your sister-in-law!"

Printed in Great Britain
by Amazon

33086123R00131